THROUGH GRANDMA'S EYES

J.E. SMYTHE

Dedicated to all the young people who are still trying to

find their way.

Everything has an end, nothing lasts forever, but

God always has a plan. Just follow his lead. – J.E. Smythe

PART I

My Permission

It was a warm, July afternoon and nineteen-year-old LaCrae James found herself sitting on the porch of her Southwest D.C. home. The neighborhood was particularly quiet that day. The air was still. There was absolutely no movement, not even a stray cat in sight. LaCrae's hands were sweaty, her stomach in a nervous knot. She was trying to work up the courage to go inside and make the ultimate announcement to her mother. She was not going back to college.

LaCrae dreamed of becoming a dancer. She didn't see why she needed college to make that dream come true. She feared she would miss her chance if she waited until after graduating to pursue it. Besides, she met a guy who directs music videos. He offered her a shot to audition as a background dancer in his next video. Her time was now. She could feel it. LaCrae believed in signs. The fact that this director guy just happened to attend the talent show at her college - the show that she had to work up her nerves to convince herself to participate in - coupled with the fact that she actually won first place, meant the universe was telling her she was ready.

All she had to do was convince her mother. LaCrae knew this was not going to be an easy task. Her mother, Francine Dupuy, or Fran for short, could be strong-willed and controlling. Fran, an elementary school teacher at a charter school in D.C. for over twenty years, had always instilled in LaCrae that education was everything. "People can take everything from you, down to the clothes on your back," Fran always said, "but they can never take the knowledge in your head." Those words constantly replayed through LaCrae's mind like a broken record. LaCrae knew her mother would never understand her decision to put college on hold to follow her dream.

From the time Fran put LaCrae in a tutu at the age of five, all she wanted to do was dance. She couldn't get enough of it. Dancing was her one addiction. When the music played, she came alive. Her body flowed with the rhythm, responding to the beat of the music as if it were the beat of her heart. She couldn't imagine her life without dance.

At first, Fran nurtured the dancer in LaCrae. She took her to every rehearsal and was always in the front row at every recital. Fran bragged about how amazing her daughter was on stage and invited everyone to come see her perform. Everyone always told LaCrae how talented she was and how she was meant to be a dancer. LaCrae relished in the attention. She danced harder with every compliment, twirled longer and faster with every hand clap.

There was a shift when she started high school. LaCrae no longer wanted to dance as a hobby. She wanted to make it her life. But her mother stopped supporting her. All Fran wanted LaCrae to do was concentrate on studying and getting into college. She always told LaCrae, "You can dance later. Right now you need to concentrate on those books."

LaCrae began to believe that her mother no longer thought she was talented. She wondered if someone suggested to Fran that she, LaCrae wasn't good enough to make it as a dancer. Fran never explained the sudden change and LaCrae never asked. While in high school, she would sneak and take dance lessons at a local studio. She was only allowed to join the high school dance team because she convinced her mother that the extracurricular activity would look great on her college applications. But now that she was away at college she didn't have to sneak anymore.

She danced as often as she wanted. She even taught dance to little girls who lived in the area. Dancing was a big part of her life. Now she was ready to make it her career.

LaCrae took two deep breaths, wiped her hands on her shorts to get rid of the sweat and slowly got up out of the chair. As she entered the house, she stopped for a moment and glanced at her reflection in the hallway mirror. Staring back at her were a set of big, hazel eyes, which perfectly accented her light brown skin. Her curly, shoulder length hair had become a mess due to the cool breeze that blew across the porch. LaCrae used her fingers as a comb and ran them through her hair to tame the tangles.

She heard her mother in the kitchen and turned to head in that direction. On the way, she stopped again, this time to admire a picture hanging on the wall of her grandparents, Charles and Mae Dupuy. It was a picture that she always liked to study, mostly to try to get a sense of who her grandparents were. LaCrae got her hazel eyes from her grandfather. After her grandfather died, her grandmother and mother hardly spoke to each other.

LaCrae always wondered what happened between them. It was difficult to imagine mother and daughter not being able to even pick up the phone for two seconds just to say hi to one another. When her grandfather was alive, LaCrae could remember going to New York all the time to visit her grandparents.

Fran got along better with her father than her mother. Fran was, without question, a daddy's girl. But since her father died, Fran rarely went back to New York. There was definitely something going on between Fran and her mother. The two of them played this crazy game. If Fran wanted to check and see how Mae was doing or if she needed something, she would call her older brother, Charles Jr., instead of speaking directly to their mother. Charles Jr.'s nickname was Charlie since he was named after their father. Charlie lived in New York, too. He was always there for his mother, never forgetting to take care of her, no matter what. Fran seemed jealous of Mae and Charlie's relationship and sometimes tried to put a wedge between them. Charlie never let her. He was devoted to his mother. But he also loved his little sister and tried his best to pacify her whenever she went on one of her rants about how awful Mae treated her.

As for Mae, whenever she needed something from Fran she also called Charlie to tell him to deliver her message to his sister. Mae hated Fran's behavior and had no patience for her antics. Keeping Fran happy was a full time job, especially since nothing seemed to make her happy. Mae refused to deal with her. When Charles was alive he babied Fran and give her all the attention she required. Mae was not going to do that.

LaCrae didn't know her grandmother that well but she did know her mother, and she always figured that the problem between her mother and grandmother had to be her mother's fault. She just expected too much out of people.

LaCrae reached the entrance of the kitchen and found her mother standing over the stove. LaCrae stood back and watched her. Fran was nearly an exact replica of Mae, from the dark brown skin tone to the naturally slender body. The only difference between Mae and Fran was that Fran had stronger, more distinctive facial features.

"Hey, Momma," LaCrae called out as she walked across the kitchen and hopped on top of the island in the middle of the room for a seat.

"Hi, baby," Fran answered, barely looking in LaCrae's direction. Fran's attention was focused on the food she was preparing and she didn't want to take her eyes off of it.

"Momma, can we talk?" LaCrae asked.

"Sure. What's up?" Fran turned around to face her daughter.

LaCrae felt the knot in her stomach again the moment her eyes met her mother's. She couldn't form the words she needed to say and she could see her mother was growing impatient. She knew she had to say something soon, because the more annoyed her mother became the less likely it would be that she would listen to what LaCrae had to say.

"Um…I met this guy who wants me to audition for him," LaCrae blurted out.

"Audition?" Fran asked, suspicious of where this conversation was going. "What do you mean 'audition'?"

"To dance," LaCrae answered. "He saw me perform at a talent show at my school and he thought I was good. So, he wants me to audition for him."

"And what exactly does he do?" Fran asked with her arms folded.

"He directs music videos," LaCrae answered, just above a whisper.

"Music videos? Like the ones that have those girls dancing half naked and shaking all their body parts?" Fran asked.

LaCrae sighed. "Momma, that's not all there is to music videos."

"Well, that's all I see," Fran replied, turning back to the stove as if she was done with the conversation.

"Well, it's not, Momma. This could be my big break!" LaCrae said, trying to convey her excitement.

"Big break for what, LaCrae?" Fran asked, still focused on cooking.

"To become a real, big time dancer," LaCrae replied.

Fran chuckled. "What you need to be concentrating on is how to be a real, big time college graduate. That should be your main focus right now, not all this silliness about music videos."

"Well, Momma, that's the thing. I think I may want to put school on hold for a while," LaCrae told her.

The moment she spoke those words the food on the stove no longer mattered. Fran flung around, on the brink of rage. "What did you just say?"

"I said I was going to put school on hold for a while," LaCrae repeated. She began to slowly push herself towards the edge of the island.

"That's what I thought you said and the answer is no," Fran replied.

"But Momma, this is my shot!" LaCrae protested. "Besides, I wasn't really asking for your permission." She knew she had to stand her ground with her mother. Otherwise, she would never be able to follow her dream.

"You're not asking my permission?" Fran asked. "So, what you're telling me is that you're grown enough to make your own decisions?"

"Yeah, Momma, that's what I'm telling you," LaCrae replied.

"Well, you know that means you also have to be able to make good decisions?" Fran continued.

LaCrae nodded. "Yes, I know that."

"And you think leaving school to go audition for a music video for a man that you don't even know is a good decision?" Fran asked.

"Momma, this is my chance and I have to take it. It may sound stupid to you, but it's what I need to do," LaCrae explained.

"No, LaCrae, it doesn't sound stupid. It *is* stupid. Let me be clear. As long as I'm supporting you, my permission is all that counts and you, my dear, do not have it," Fran said.

LaCrae was angry with her mother for completely ignoring what she wanted and what she felt was good for her. She jumped down off the kitchen island, crossing the room to stand toe-to-toe with Fran. She was determined to stand up for herself. LaCrae knew she had to make her see her as an adult who was capable of making her own decisions.

"I'm doing this, Momma, no matter what you say," LaCrae said, giving her mother the sternest look she could muster.

But Fran didn't flinch. She looked her daughter straight in the eye and without blinking said, "Then you'll need to go upstairs, pack your bags and be out in the morning."

Fran's eyes followed LaCrae as she turned to walk away. She waited for LaCrae to come back and apologize. But LaCrae would not give her the satisfaction. She refused to turn around. If she did, her mother would declare herself the winner and that would be the end of any hope LaCrae ever had of becoming a dancer.

LaCrae hurried to her room and laid across her bed. She had absolutely no idea what to do next. Fran had called her bluff and it looked like she was stuck.

New York

It was 7:00 a.m. the next morning and LaCrae was on a bus from D.C. to New York, where her audition was scheduled to be held in two weeks. She hadn't planned on going to New York this early but she figured she didn't have a choice. She had to leave and take a chance.

She used nearly all the money she had in her bank account to buy the bus ticket and had no idea what she would do once her money ran out. The last thing she would do is call her mother to ask for help. When Fran told her to get out, she did. LaCrae didn't even wait for her to wake up, she just left. Her plan was to call and tell her where she was once she figured everything out.

And that was the extent of her plan. She didn't know where she was going or where she was going to live. She'd heard crazy stories about young girls just like her heading to New York with big dreams only to end up on the streets. LaCrae didn't want that for herself. Working on the streets for some wanna-be pimp was not a part of her dreams.

She sat back in her seat and stared out the window, watching as the bus passed cars and trees. For the first time since the night before she questioned her decision. Maybe her mother was right. This was the first big move she'd ever made on her own and she realized it could all go so wrong, so fast. The last thing she wanted was to go back to D.C. broke and having to hear her say "I told you so."

$$* * *$$

Fran woke up around 9:00 a.m. She listened carefully for the sound of LaCrae moving around in the house. When she didn't hear anything she got out of bed and went straight to LaCrae's bedroom. She slowly opened the door, hoping to find LaCrae safely tucked in her bed. But what she found was a perfectly made bed in an empty room.

"LaCrae!" Fran called. "LaCrae!" But there was no answer. She walked around frantically upstairs, opening every door to every room, but they were all empty. Fran ran down the stairs and called out again,

"LaCrae! Where are you?!" Again, only silence. Fran sat down on the sofa in the living room. LaCrae was gone. She had defied her.

Her daughter had always been a good girl and never gave her any problems. She always had strict control over LaCrae and this was the first time LaCrae had challenged her. She had no clue where her daughter was going or what kind of trouble she was about to get herself into. She got up to get the phone to dial LaCrae's cell number, but decided against it. She thought it may be time for some tough love.

LaCrae had to learn why she was so hard on her. She had to learn that the world is no place for an uneducated woman. No matter how talented you are, the world will chew you up and spit you out if you're not smart enough to know when someone means you harm. All she ever wanted for her daughter was for her to be a strong, independent woman. She never wanted her out there chasing after a phantom dream like her father.

LaCrae's father, a jazz musician, left when LaCrae was barely in elementary school. He eventually came back, but left again for good when LaCrae was about to enter high school. Fran vowed right then and there that no one else under her roof would ever get caught up in the unattainable. She had raised LaCrae all on her own and up until now she thought she'd done a pretty good job. But now LaCrae thought she knew better, and Fran was going to let her go it alone. Though it would be hard, she had to back off and let LaCrae fall.

***

The bus finally reached Penn Station in New York City about four hours after she boarded. LaCrae got off, dragging a big duffle bag behind her. She had arrived. "Now what?" she asked herself.

LaCrae took out her cell phone and looked through it. She wasn't sure what she was looking for. She just hoped that something would pop up. Then, something did. There, staring back at her, was her grandmother's address. For some reason LaCrae completely forgot about her living in New York. What better way to stick it to her mother than to go stay with the one person that knew just how to make her mother miserable?

She dialed her grandmother's number, but nobody answered. LaCrae had no idea how to get to her house. She thought about taking a cab, but her grandmother lived in

Harlem and something told her that the cost of getting a cab from Manhattan to Harlem would be a stretch for her already non-existent budget.

She saw a girl who looked to be around her age. LaCrae went over and asked her which would be the best way to get to Harlem. The girl gave LaCrae the directions for which train to take and soon LaCrae was standing on the underground platform waiting for the train to arrive. The train in New York was different from the D.C. metro. Everything was so dirty and it was much more crowded. LaCrae remembered hearing once that when in New York, you should always keep your belongings close to you. So she took out the long strap for her duffel bag and hooked the strap to the bag. Then she put it over her head and across her shoulder. The train slowly came to screeching stop in front of her and she cautiously walked through the doors as they opened. LaCrae took a seat and held on to a pole as the train began to move.

After taking two trains she still had to walk a couple of blocks to her grandmother's house. As LaCrae walked, she noticed how many people were out on the streets. There seemed to be a convenience store on every corner and people were just hanging around. The atmosphere was busy and noisy. LaCrae wondered how her grandmother could live around here. Not that D.C. was any better as far the noise was concerned, but at least people seemed to have a purpose. They were going somewhere and doing something.

Finally, LaCrae reached the steps leading to her grandmother's brownstone. She climbed to the top of the stairs and rang the bell. Nobody came to the door. LaCrae looked through the window to see if she could see her moving around, but the inside of the house looked dark. LaCrae banged on the door in case she was upstairs and couldn't hear the doorbell.

"Can I help you?" a young Hispanic man asked as he emerged from underneath the stairs. LaCrae figured he was about her age or maybe a little bit older. She didn't know who he was or why he was there.

"I'm looking for Mae Dupuy," LaCrae said to the man.

"Is she expecting you?" he asked.

"No, but I think she would be happy to see me just the same," LaCrae said, offended that some stranger was questioning her. "Anyway, who are you?"

"Well, that depends," he said.

"On what?" LaCrae asked, becoming more aggravated.

"On who you are," he replied with a hint of a smile.

"I'm LaCrae James, Mae's granddaughter. Your turn," LaCrae said. Her attitude seemed to amuse the man.

"Hi, LaCrae James. I'm Julio, I live in the basement apartment." Julio extended his hand for LaCrae to shake, but she just stared at him with her arms folded.

"Where's my grandmother?" she asked.

Julio chuckled and pointed, "She's at the bodega on the corner. If you want, you can leave your stuff here and go find her. I'll watch it for you."

"I don't know you. You might take my stuff and run away with it," LaCrae replied.

Julio laughed. "You don't have to worry about me taking your stuff. I would never do that. Besides, here comes Ms. Mae now." Julio nodded his head in the direction over LaCrae's shoulder.

She turned to see a gray-haired woman, dressed like a seventy-year-old but walked as if she were only twenty.

The woman made her way up the street pushing a two wheel shopping cart in front of her. It was as if the whole neighborhood knew her. As she passed people they all stopped to smile at her and say hello. Julio jumped off the porch and ran up to LaCrae's grandmother, taking the cart from her hands.

When Mae got to the porch, she looked straight up at LaCrae on the top of the steps. LaCrae had forgotten how pretty she was. She had smooth, soft, dark brown skin that lacked any hint of wrinkles. LaCrae wanted to run right into her arms as she looked at her with those big, brown eyes. But instead, she stood there, wondering whether her grandmother even recognized her. It had been so long since they last saw each other.

"Child, what do you have on?" Mae asked as she gave LaCrae's clothes the once over.

LaCrae, dressed in fitted skinny jeans, sneakers and a white midriff t-shirt, suddenly felt uncomfortable. "What's wrong with it?" LaCrae asked as she tugged at her t-shirt, hoping it would suddenly become longer.

"Lord, you look like you about to go to the club. You come from D.C. looking like that?" Mae asked as she began to climb up the six steps. Julio followed close behind carrying the shopping cart.

As Mae reached the top of the stairs, she took another look at LaCrae. "Well, don't just stand there. Give me a hug, child."

LaCrae threw her arms around her grandmother and held on tight. When she finally let go, Mae held LaCrae's shoulders, staring into her hazel eyes as if they were something she'd never seen before and may never see again.

"Well, come on, child. Let's go inside," Mae instructed, her eyes still on LaCrae.

LaCrae wondered what seemed to mesmerize her grandmother. Perhaps she was just trying to take her in after not seeing her for such a long-time. After all, she was doing the same thing, looking at her grandmother from head to toe, comparing her to the woman in the pictures on the walls at home.

"Julio, baby, leave those groceries right there and help LaCrae with her things. Show her to that first bedroom at the top of the stairs," Mae said as they walked into the living room.

"No, Grandma, that's alright. I got it," LaCrae said, grabbing her duffle bag before Julio had a chance to take it.

"Oh, Lord. You new generation women need to learn how to let a man be a gentleman," Mae said, giving LaCrae a stern look.

LaCrae's mother had given her that same look many times and she knew what it meant. She handed the duffle bag to Julio, who gave her a smile and a nod.

He led LaCrae up the stairs. The bedroom was empty except for a full size bed and a dresser. The bed was not made, but the sheets were folded in a neat stack at the edge of the bed. LaCrae walked over to the window and pulled the curtains aside. She had the perfect view of the street below in front of the house.

"I'll put your stuff right here," Julio said as he placed LaCrae's duffle bag on the bare mattress.

"Thank you," LaCrae replied, still peering through the window.

"Hey, if you need anything...you know, help getting around, just let me know," Julio said.

LaCrae turned around to look at him. "I can take care of myself. I don't need your help getting around."

Julio chuckled and left the room, closing the door behind him.

✳✳✳

Julio had never met a girl as stubborn or intent on being as mean as LaCrae. It tickled him a little. LaCrae was beautiful, but he was just getting out of a miserable relationship and had no intention of pursuing her. He could see the innocence in her face and knew that she was going to get in over her head at some point. He thought it best to keep a close eye on her.

Julio knew all too well what kind of trouble a young girl could get into on the streets of New York. His older sister ran away from home when she was sixteen and ended up prostituting herself for drugs. At the time, Julio was too young to help her. A part of him couldn't blame her for running away. Their home life was no picnic. Their mother's only focus was to get and keep a man, and if that meant forgetting about her kids every now and then, so be it. His sister used to take care of him and their three siblings. Then one day, she just up and left.

When Julio was old enough, he went looking for her and found her in a crack house. He did everything he could to help her but nothing worked. She died of a drug overdose when he was a sophomore in high school. It was then that Julio decided that he had to be an example to his remaining siblings. He graduated high school at the top of his class and then went on to college. All the while he worked and supported himself and his siblings.

He always felt obligated to make sure no one else he knew or loved ended up like his sister. So far he'd done a pretty decent job. He got his mom to realize how important it is for her to focus on her kids. She now provides a safe home for Julio's siblings, for which Julio pays the rent.

He tip-toed back to the room and quietly opened the door just enough to peek inside. LaCrae was curled up on the bed, fast asleep. Before turning away he took another look at her toned, slim body and marveled at her beauty. He could tell she was something special.

You Only Have the Summer

LaCrae woke up to the smell of something frying in the kitchen. As she made her way downstairs she could hear people talking. At first she thought it was her grandmother and Julio, but the male voice was different. LaCrae couldn't tell who it was until she came into the kitchen and saw her grandmother at the stove, her Uncle Charlie sitting at the kitchen table, and Uncle Charlie's wife, Aunt Esther, at the sink washing dishes.

"Well, would you look at who decided to get up?!" Uncle Charlie shouted.

"Hi, Uncle Charlie!" LaCrae walked over to give him a hug. She hadn't seen him in a while, but all of her memories of Uncle Charlie were so pleasant. She really missed him.

Uncle Charlie gave her a big squeeze and a kiss on the cheek. "You have grown into such a beautiful young lady."

"She sure has," said Aunt Esther, as she came over to wrap LaCrae in her arms.

Uncle Charlie had been married to Aunt Esther for as long as LaCrae could remember. They had three kids - one in law school, one pre-med, and the other was the star football player for his college team. Uncle Charlie was the CEO of a major financial firm in Manhattan and Aunt Esther was the head of medical research at the top hospital in New York. They were the picture of perfection but were never snobby or pompous. They genuinely cared about people and always had a smile and hug for anyone who came around. That's why LaCrae loved them.

But Fran didn't get along with Aunt Esther. Once, LaCrae heard her say that Aunt Esther came along and took her spot. LaCrae could recall Fran's exact words: "Momma does not need me anymore. She's found a brand new daughter in Esther. All thanks to Charlie, the good child." LaCrae didn't know if she was being sarcastic, but she did know that her mother only spoke to Aunt Esther when it was absolutely necessary. Their conversations were always short and to the point.

"Come on, take a seat." Uncle Charlie directed her to the chair across the table from him. "How have you been?"

"I'm alright, I guess," LaCrae answered.

"That's good. You know, I spoke with your mother and she's not too happy with you right now," Uncle Charlie said.

"Well, I'm not too happy with her either, Uncle Charlie," LaCrae replied.

"I heard your mother's side of the story. Why don't you tell me yours?" he asked.

LaCrae looked around the room and noticed that her Aunt Esther had moved closer to stand by the kitchen table. But her grandmother kept right on cooking as if nothing was happening. LaCrae was nervous about sharing her side because from her experience, adults always stuck together. But despite what she felt, she told them almost everything. She left out the part about going to meet with a director to audition for a music video. She figured one or all of them would try to talk her out of it.

When she finished explaining she sat back and waited for them to flip out like her mother did. Instead,

Aunt Esther sat down at the table. "Sweetheart, are you sure this is what you want to do?"

"I'm sure, Aunt Esther. All I want is to take a shot at following my dreams," LaCrae told her.

"You do realize that this is not going to be easy?" Uncle Charlie asked.

LaCrae nodded. "I know. But shouldn't I at least try?"

Uncle Charlie squeezed her hand, giving her a wink and a smile. Then he turned and asked, "Mama, what do you think?"

"I think I don't want any problems with Fran," Mae answered.

"I'll talk to Fran, Mama. I'll tell her to at least let LaCrae stay through the summer," Uncle Charlie said. He turned back to LaCrae, "But you only have the summer. If you want to stay past the summer, you're going to have to get a job and make your own way."

LaCrae jumped up and threw her arms around her uncle. She knew that if anybody could get through to her mother it would be Uncle Charlie. The only concern

LaCrae had was her grandmother, who was silent and made no comments. She was difficult to read and LaCrae wondered if this was related to some of the issues between her mother and grandmother. But those issues belonged to them. LaCrae didn't care if her grandmother didn't say a word to her the whole summer. As long as LaCrae was able to stay in New York, she knew that her dream of becoming a professional dancer was within reach.

✱✱✱

After dinner, Charlie and Esther said their goodbyes and left. They stood at the bottom of the steps outside of Mae's brownstone. They looked at each other and sighed, both aware of the fact that Fran's reaction to LaCrae staying in New York was not going to be good. Esther ran her fingers across Charlie's handsome face. He was nearly 6 feet tall and his complexion was so light that people often mistook him for a white man. His captivating blue eyes caused Esther to fall head-over-heels in love when they first met in college. In the beginning, Esther could never decide which parent her husband most resembled. She assumed he was a perfect combination of both his mother and father.

Charlie gently took his wife's caramel colored hand in his own and softly kissed her palm. The gesture made Esther smile.

"So," Esther said, "are you going to give Fran a call now?"

"I prefer to be in the comfort of my own home close to my Scotch before calling her," Charlie said with a smile, and led his wife by the hand to their car.

Damn

The next morning LaCrae woke up to the sounds of people talking below her window and cars honking as they drove down the street. She picked up her unpacked duffle bag from the floor and pulled out clothes to wear. In her haste to pack, she forgot a few things, including a towel and toothbrush.

LaCrae went to her grandmother's room and knocked on the door. There was no response. She turned the knob.

"Grandma, are you awake?" She entered her grandmother's room. It was full of clusters of trinkets, yet it was neat. Everything had its own place. Pictures of her grandparents hung on the walls. There were several of her grandfather, which LaCrae thought was odd. She knew people kept photos of deceased loved ones on display, but she didn't understand why her grandmother needed so many.

A table in the corner was filled with candles positioned in a circle, and in the middle stood a picture of LaCrae's grandfather. She went over and picked it up. This photo was different from all the others she had seen, including the one that hung on the wall at her own house. In this picture he was young and handsome with slick, black hair. His smile was warm and inviting. It was a black and white photo, decades old but well kept. The black frame was shiny and dust free. LaCrae could see why her grandmother kept this particular picture in such a special place. Her grandfather's eyes were alert and staring right at her, as if he could see her.

LaCrae felt a little uneasy once she realized that the photo had been positioned so that her grandfather was facing the bed. She wondered if it was odd to have eyes staring at you while you slept. She wondered how her grandmother could be so comfortable having a dead man be the first thing she sees when she wakes up and the last thing she sees when she goes to bed.

"You looking for something?"

Startled by the sound of her grandmother's voice, LaCrae nearly dropped the photo. Mae quickly took it out of her hands and placed it gently back in its position on the table.

"Sorry, Grandma. I just wanted a towel and a toothbrush. I didn't…I'm sorry," LaCrae said, worried she was angry.

"I already put both on your bed."

Her grandmother was even harder to read than she initially thought. LaCrae left the room without saying anything else.

She took her time getting dressed, giving her grandmother time to cool off in case she was upset. When LaCrae finally went downstairs Mae was in the living room, sitting in the window seat. She was looking outside but her mind was a million miles away. Soft music played in the background. LaCrae didn't recognize the singer's voice.

"Hey, Grandma," LaCrae said cautiously.

"Hey. There's some breakfast for you in the kitchen," Mae replied.

"Thanks, but I'm not really hungry," LaCrae said.

"Go on and eat something, child. Breakfast is important," Mae said absently, her eyes still focused on the window, her mind far away.

LaCrae, assuming her grandmother was still mad, sat down on the sofa across from the window seat. "Grandma, I'm really sorry."

"For what?" Mae asked, finally turning in LaCrae's direction.

"For going in your room. I promise I wasn't snooping," LaCrae said.

"Oh, that's alright, child. There's no need to watch your step in this house," Mae said.

"Can I ask you a question?" LaCrae asked.

"What's that?"

"Why do you have his picture like that? The one on the table by your bed."

Mae's eyes were on LaCrae, but her mind went to that faraway place again. Then she returned just as quickly to the present. "Well, how else can you talk to someone if they're not looking at you?"

LaCrae was afraid for her grandmother and wondered if she was in the beginning stages of Alzheimer's. After all, she was in her seventies. That's the only thing that could explain her thinking that she could talk to someone who's been dead for years.

Mae suspected the type of thoughts that were running through her granddaughter's head. "Don't look at me like I'm crazy, child. I didn't say he talks back. It's just that when you've shared a life with someone, it's hard not to run and tell them how your day was. Some people may think that's crazy of me but I choose to believe that he's up in heaven listening."

LaCrae smiled at her. She vaguely remembered hearing stories about her grandparents having a fairytale love. But LaCrae didn't believe in that type of love. It was a struggle for her own parents just to be in the same room, and her father had put all thoughts of her and her mother out of his mind long ago.

According to Fran, Charles and Mae didn't have such a fairytale life. During one of Fran's angry rants she blurted out to LaCrae that Charles may not be her father. Fran suspected that the reason Mae didn't treat her as well as she treated Charlie was because she wasn't the child of her one, true love. "But my daddy never treated me differently," Fran had said. "I was his little princess. That's why I loved that man."

But based on the way Mae talked about her husband, LaCrae could not imagine another man interfering with their love. There was no way a woman who talked to a picture of her dead husband every night would have allowed another man to touch her. LaCrae concluded there was no truth to her mother's angry rant.

There was no stopping Fran's mouth when she was furious. She said the most outrageous things. Fran's sharp insults were hurtful to LaCrae, but apparently they were not reserved just for her. LaCrae wondered how her mother could say such a thing about her grandmother, especially since it was obvious her grandparents loved each other very much. Their kind of love was rare and untouchable. What was the secret to finding that type of love?

LaCrae, once again aware of the music coming from the record player, asked "Who's that, Grandma? Some old jazz singer?"

"Old, yes," Mae chuckled. "It's someone you've never even heard of." She smiled at LaCrae, then got up and turned off the record player before walking up the stairs.

* * *

After breakfast LaCrae headed outside to the front stoop. She found Julio ending a conversation with a girl who spoke Spanish. As the girl walked away, she looked over her shoulder and shot a dirty look at LaCrae.

LaCrae sat down on the steps as Julio came up towards her. "Good morning, LaCrae James," he said.

"Who was that? One of your baby mamas?" LaCrae asked with a smirk.

"Baby mamas?" Julio asked, offended. "Is that the type of dude you think I am?"

"I don't know what type of dude you are," LaCrae answered.

"That's strange because by the way you act, you would think that you not only knew me but that I've done something wrong to you," Julio said.

"Well, I don't know you and don't really want to. Besides, why are you always hanging around?"

"I hang around because I live here."

"That's not what I mean. You make yourself way too comfortable in my grandmother's house. You're a tenant, not a roommate," she clarified.

"All I'm doing is trying to help your grandmother. I think she's a nice lady," he explained.

"Yeah right. I know all about you New York guys," LaCrae said.

"Really?" he asked. "And what do you know about us 'New York guys'?"

"I know that you guys are always up to something. Ya'll like that street life," she informed him. "You probably targeted my grandmother because she's old and alone. Well, I'm here now and I'm not about to let you take advantage of her."

Julio let out a loud laugh. "You know, something tells me I don't want to take you on, so let me explain. I didn't target your grandmother. Your Uncle Charlie offered me the basement apartment. He didn't want Ms. Mae in this big house all by herself and he knew I was in the market for a reasonable priced place to live."

"How do you know my uncle?" LaCrae asked.

"I met him when I interned at his office while in college."

She was taken aback by this information. Her tone softened. "You're in college?"

"Graduated. I'm working on my master's in Business," Julio answered.

"Oh," she replied, lowering her eyes.

"Does that 'oh' mean you're going to cut me a little bit of slack?" Julio asked, smiling.

"No," LaCrae said. "It means that maybe I was a little bit hasty in my judgment of you. Sorry."

Julio smiled again, got up and walked down the stairs towards his apartment.

For the first time LaCrae allowed herself to really look at him. He wasn't bad looking. He was tall, not quite like a basketball player, but he easily could have been 6 feet. His hair was jet black and wavy. He was muscular like an athlete, but his muscles weren't overly large. He looked as though he had the right amount of strength to handle anything that came his way.

As he gripped the handrail, LaCrae stared in amazement at his white t-shirt stretched across his toned chest. He managed to impress her with his smarts and his looks, but LaCrae was not going to let physical attraction distract her from making sure he didn't take advantage of her grandmother. When she got up to go back inside she leaned over the rail to catch one last glimpse.

"Damn."

That Kind of Dancer

After a few days in New York, LaCrae realized her audition was fast approaching. She was starting to get nervous. It was important to show everyone how talented she was. She had to prove them all wrong because it was obvious they didn't think she knew what she was doing. LaCrae could tell her aunt and uncle were patronizing her. Her mother never called. She was just waiting for LaCrae to fail and come back home begging for forgiveness. But mostly, LaCrae could tell by the way her grandmother walked around the house humming and not saying a word. LaCrae refused to give any of them the satisfaction of being right.

She noticed a community center about a block away from the house. LaCrae put on dance clothes and went to the center to ask if they would let her use one of their rooms to practice. When she arrived, the woman at the front desk asked, "You're a dancer?"

"Yeah," LaCrae answered.

"For how long?" the woman asked.

"All my life," LaCrae said. "I've been taking dance lessons since I was little."

The woman was intrigued. "Really? Do you teach?"

"Yeah…a little. Just for a few kids," LaCrae slowly replied.

"Well, I'll say. That's something," she said.

"Why are you asking?"

"We were thinking about starting a dance class but couldn't find a teacher," she explained. "Would you be interested?"

LaCrae firmly declined. "Oh, no. I'm getting ready for an audition. I don't have time to teach."

"Wow, I'm so sorry. I should have known since you're here to practice. I heard the Dance Academy is having open auditions for new students," she said.

"No. I'm not a student. I have an audition for a music video," LaCrae proudly declared.

"Oh…you're *that* kind of dancer. I get it. No, that's not what we're looking for in a teacher. But you're welcome to use one of our empty classrooms downstairs. Just pick one," she said.

LaCrae turned and walked away, her confidence deflated by the woman's words. The way she said 'you're *that* kind of dancer' made LaCrae feel cheap. Like her talent didn't matter. Obviously people had their own beliefs about dancers in music videos. It was then that she realized that she had to show more than just her family. She was not '*that* kind of dancer.' She was a great dancer. Once she landed the spot in the video, they would all know that she is truly a star.

✳✳✳

In her rush to leave D.C. LaCrae realized she didn't bring any music for dance practice. Instead, she relied on the melodies that played in her head. She closed her eyes and began to move. She felt completely free as her body moved through air and space. Soon, her mind left her body as she floated high in the clouds. Nothing else mattered. She was at peace.

The sound of loud clapping brought her back to reality.

"I'm sorry to interrupt, but I wanted to bring this old CD player for you. There are a few CDs in there. But it doesn't seem like you need it," said the woman from the front desk.

"Thank you. I'll take a look," LaCrae replied.

"You are really good."

"Thanks."

"It's a shame," the woman sighed.

"What is?" LaCrae asked

"That you're not a student. I think the Dance Academy is the perfect place for you," she said.

"Well, I'm not," LaCrae said, slightly annoyed.

"If you change your mind, I can find the information for you," the woman offered.

"I won't," LaCrae replied.

The woman started to leave the room but paused and turned back. "By the way, my name is Domonique."

"I'm -"

"LaCrae," Dominique interrupted. "I already know who you are." Domonique smiled, winked, and walked out of the room.

LaCrae noticed the confidence in Domonique's stride, her elegant demeanor. Domonique looked to be around the same age as LaCrae's mother but she had a young spirit. She wore her hair in dreadlocks and dressed in African attire, but she didn't have an African accent. Domonique had an air of calm about her. She appeared to be Afro-centric, one of those people who seemed to be much more evolved than everyone else. She spoke through a smile and tilted her head in acknowledgment of your presence. LaCrae hated those kind of people. They were so annoying, always acting like they had all the answers or that they knew better than anyone else. As if being plain and ordinary was so wrong. She didn't need dreadlocks or kente cloth to prove that she was centered and intellectual. She didn't need or care about Domonique's advice.

LaCrae turned her attention to the CDs. She picked out a few that she liked and practiced like she had never practiced before. From that day on, LaCrae went to the community center to rehearse, and Domonique always made sure there was an available room and music for her.

***

The day before the audition LaCrae went to the community center for one last practice. Domonique stopped her as she walked in. "Hey, LaCrae. I know you're not interested but a friend gave me this flyer. Apparently the Dance Academy auditions will be held at the Apollo Theater in a few weeks. You should think about it."

"Domonique, I told you I'm not interested," LaCrae replied.

"I know. But it doesn't hurt to have a look." Domonique pushed the flyer into LaCrae's hand.

LaCrae took the flyer, walked away, and added Domonique to the list of people who didn't believe in her dream. Just another person she had to prove wrong. No one was going to make her think she couldn't land a spot in the music video. She was good enough and she didn't understand why everyone around her didn't think so. But all that mattered is that she believed in herself. LaCrae went into a room and danced harder than she had during the past few days. Now, she was finally ready.

As she left the center, she made sure to avoid Domonique. She didn't want to hear one more thing about the damn Dance Academy audition. She had her own plans and going to the Dance Academy was not a part of them.

When she got to her grandmother's house she saw Julio talking to a Latina girl with a big ass, dressed like she should be on the corner working for her rent. Julio was smiling, obviously enjoying her company. LaCrae tried to walk past them but Julio stopped her. "Hey, LaCrae."

"Hey," LaCrae answered.

"Sonya, I'll catch up with you later," Julio told the girl.

"Aight," she said, rolling her eyes at LaCrae as she walked off.

LaCrae mentally noted that this was a different girl than the one from a few days ago and concluded Julio was a player.

"How's everything going?" Julio asked.

"Good. You didn't have to send your girlfriend away," LaCrae said.

"She's not my girlfriend," Julio said, smiling.

"Could have fooled me."

"She's not really my type," Julio said. "Anyway, I didn't realize how good of a dancer you were."

LaCrae was confused. "What are you talking about?"

"I saw you at the community center. I didn't want to bother you, so I just watched you dance for a while. You're really good," Julio said.

"Thanks." LaCrae said, as she walked into the house, blushing from his compliment.

She looked around downstairs for her grandmother but she was nowhere to be found. She thought of knocking on her bedroom door but remembered what happened the last time. Still, LaCrae felt like she should check on her. After all, they lived in the same house and hadn't seen each other all day.

LaCrae went upstairs, slowly opened her grandmother's bedroom door and found her lying on the bed. She quietly walked over to the bed and pulled the covers over her. To her shock, she noticed her grandmother's hair resting on the nightstand. She always assumed her hair was real, not a wig. She had the exact same hairstyle in all of her pictures. LaCrae gently pushed back the scarf on her grandmother's head. She was surprised to see chunks of hair were missing. After moving the scarf back in place, LaCrae left the room.

She went to her bedroom to put together the perfect outfit to wear to the audition. But the image of her grandmother's missing hair kept flashing through her mind. She hoped that her grandmother was alright, but most of all she hoped whatever was going on with her was not hereditary.

✳✳✳

Julio sat on the steps of the brownstone, deep in thought. There was so much more he wanted to say to LaCrae but couldn't get the words out. She intrigued him and kept him on his toes. He liked that. He couldn't get her out of his head. Memories of her gliding across the floor as she danced brought a smile to his face. She looked amazing. He had lied to her. The reason he didn't interrupt her dancing wasn't that he didn't want to disturb her. It was that he didn't want her to stop. She looked like an angel as she turned and leaped through the air. The way she mixed ballet and hip-hop dance moves impressed him. Her command of her body was unlike anything he'd ever seen before.

He was about to get up and leave when Sonya came back. Julio rolled his eyes at the sight of her. Ever since he and his ex-girlfriend broke up women had been throwing themselves at him. Julio was a catch. He was gorgeous, educated, and on his way to becoming successful.

"What is it Sonya?" Julio asked.

"I forgot to ask you if you wanted to come with me to this party tonight," Sonya said in her blended Puerto Rican New Yorker accent.

"No. I have some work to do," Julio declined. "But thank you."

"Come on, papi, you can't spend the rest of your life working," Sonya said with a smirk.

"I know, but not tonight," Julio said.

"Ok, papi, but if you change your mind you know where to find me." Sonya turned and strutted up the street.

Julio watched as she walked away. He looked up at LaCrae's window before going back down to his apartment.

Q

It was the day of the audition. LaCrae woke up early and got dressed. She had done her homework and discovered exactly how to get to Brooklyn from Harlem. She quietly made her way downstairs, assuming Mae was not awake yet. But by the time she got to the bottom she saw her grandmother sitting in the living room, the same faraway look in her eyes as before.

"Grandma?" LaCrae called out.

"Oh…LaCrae…I didn't hear you get up," Mae said. "Are you going somewhere?"

"Um…I just got this thing I need to do," LaCrae replied.

"Oh…a thing. Right. Well, I wish you good luck with your thing," Mae said.

"Thanks," LaCrae said and ran out the front door.

Mae knew full well what LaCrae had to do. Domonique had updated her on everything from the audition to LaCrae's talent as a dancer. Domonique desperately wanted Mae to convince LaCrae to try out for the performing arts academy, but Mae declined. It wasn't her place to tell LaCrae what to do or how to live her life. As far as Mae was concerned, people do what they think is right even when it's wrong. Far be it for Mae to be the one who told LaCrae that she was headed for disaster.

✳✳✳

It felt like it took forever to get to the audition site, but she finally made it. LaCrae walked into the building and found the lobby filled with girls who didn't even look like dancers. They were all half naked with their private parts hanging all over the place. Some of them had gigantic asses and big boobs that jiggled with every step.

LaCrae went over to a woman sitting behind a desk. "Hi, I'm here to audition."

"Here's your number, have a seat," the woman said, throwing a piece of paper at her with the number 23 written on it.

LaCrae sat next to a girl who alternated between filing her nails and fixing her hair. The girl seemed to be more interested in grooming than getting ready for an audition. LaCrae looked her up and down, noticing that she had on fishnet stockings, short shorts, a tank top that barely covered her boobs and heels that had to be about eight inches tall. LaCrae looked down at her own outfit - sweatpants, an off the shoulder t-shirt, and sneakers. She suddenly felt underdressed and wondered if she was supposed to dress like the girl next to her. This was LaCrae's first time auditioning as an actual dancer. She had no idea how to dress or act.

"Hi," LaCrae said to the girl. She was hoping to get some information on how the audition process worked.

"Hey," the girl replied, still filing her nails and only glancing at LaCrae.

"Is this your first audition?" LaCrae asked.

"No girl. I've been to a couple of these things," the girl answered.

"Wow. How long have you been dancing?" LaCrae asked.

"Dancing? How you know I'm a dancer?" asked the girl, defensive.

"Cause you're here. I just assumed that you dance," LaCrae explained.

"Oh. Well yeah, I do," the girl said. "Let's see, I was at Baby Doll's for about two years and now I've been at Juicy's for about a year. So I guess I've been dancing for three years…yeah that sounds about right."

LaCrae froze as it dawned on her that the girl was a stripper. She wondered why a stripper would be at a dance audition. It wasn't that kind of dancing. At least she hoped it wasn't. LaCrae had a few more questions but before she could get the words out she heard a woman call "Twenty-three? Number twenty-three?"

LaCrae got up and followed the woman into a room that looked like a dance studio. The room was filled with thuggish looking guys who were smoking and laughing as though they were hanging out at one of their boy's houses rather than an audition. As she entered the room, they all turned their attention towards her. She felt as though their eyes were undressing her and she could feel them touching her exposed body. For the first time since she arrived at the audition, LaCrae was afraid. She just wanted to get out of there. But she knew all she needed to focus on was dancing. The sooner she could do her routine, the sooner she could leave.

"What's your name, ma?" one of the guys asked her.

"LaCrae," she answered softly.

"Alright. Do me a favor, ma. Give me your sexiest walk," he said.

"My what?" LaCrae asked, confused.

"Just go back against that wall and walk towards the front, and be really sexy," the guy answered.

LaCrae did what she was asked but she didn't know if her walk was sexy or not. She tried to do it like a dancer would, graceful and sensual, but she had no clue whether that was sexy. When she finished, the guy got up and walked over to her. Then he walked around her looking her up and down. Again, she was afraid. It was just her in a room full of men and she was sure they were smoking on something more than just cigarettes. But the guy stood beside her and looked back at the other men and asked "What y'all think?" The men nodded.

The guy went back to his seat and said to LaCrae "Aight, ma, thanks for coming. Go see homegirl at the desk."

LaCrae turned to leave the room, wondering why they didn't ask her to dance. She didn't know if this was just the first step in the audition process. Were they going to have her dance later? She had no clue what any of this meant. As LaCrae entered the hallway she ran into the director who had invited her to the audition.

"Hey!" LaCrae said, excited to finally see a face she recognized.

"Hey! It's shorty from D.C. How did it go in there?" he asked.

"I'm not really sure. They just asked me to walk and then told me to go see the girl at the desk," LaCrae replied.

"Oh, well hold up for a sec let me go in and find out." Then he left LaCrae standing alone in the hall.

When he returned he said, "Good news, Miss D.C. You got it."

"I did?!" LaCrae asked, surprised.

"Of course you did. You bad, girl. I told you." he said.

"Oh…wow…thank you. What do I have to do next? I mean, where's the video shoot?" LaCrae asked.

"You know what, where you staying?" he asked.

"With my grandmother in Harlem," LaCrae replied.

"Cool. I'm about to bounce, so why don't I take you home and we can discuss all that on the way," he offered. "Is that aight with you?"

"Yeah, sure," LaCrae replied.

Before they left, the director opened the door to the audition studio and yelled to the guys inside, "Yo! I'm out. Hit me up if you need me."

"Aight, Q. See you later man," one of them replied.

"Q?" LaCrae asked.

"Yeah, that's what they call me. My real name is Quincy, but nobody but my mother calls me that," Q said with a chuckle. "I remember your name was hard as hell."

She smiled. "LaCrae."

"That's pretty." Q grinned and led her out of the building.

Have Fun

Riding in Q's big, black Escalade with tinted windows and enormous rims made LaCrae feel like she had finally arrived. Everything was going exactly as she had planned. So much for people thinking that she didn't know what she was doing. She'd finally proven them all wrong. Her plan was working and she was excited. LaCrae knew without a doubt that this first video would lead to more, and pretty soon she'd be choreographing dance routines for all the stars. Her excitement grew as Q talked about the video and how much potential he thought she had. He told her that she could be a star and LaCrae believed him. Finally, someone saw what she saw in herself and he was willing to help her reach her goals. He seemed to be the only person in her life who wasn't discouraging her from doing what she loved to do the most.

As Q's Escalade pulled up in front of her grandmother's house, LaCrae saw Julio sitting on the steps again. But this time it looked like he was waiting for someone. LaCrae couldn't wait for him to see her with Q, this buff, dark-skinned brother who obviously had a lot of money and influence. She couldn't wait for all of them to see that she'd made it. She was officially a dancer and someone like Q actually saw her potential.

"So, this you?" Q asked.

"Yes, this is my grandmother's house," LaCrae answered.

"Listen, how about I come by later tonight and take you to this club. It's the spot and there'll be a lot of people that I think you should meet," Q said.

LaCrae nodded. "Yeah, I'd like that."

"Cool. I'll see you later and wear something really sexy for me, aight?" Q said.

"Ok," LaCrae said with a smile.

She didn't know if she'd packed anything sexy, at least not club sexy. LaCrae immediately began to wonder what she could wear that would impress Q and the people he wanted her to meet. The anticipation of meeting people who could possibly change her life was almost too much for her to handle. She could feel her heart begin to race and her palms start to sweat. It was finally happening for her and she trusted Q to guide her career.

As LaCrae opened the door to get out of Q's truck, Julio stood up. He didn't look at her but past her at the person in the truck. LaCrae closed the door and waved at Q as he drove off. She turned to face Julio who gave her a disapproving look. But LaCrae was not going to be bothered by what Julio thought. She was pleased with herself and nobody was going to ruin that feeling.

"So, you made a new friend?" Julio asked as she walked up the stairs.

"He's not a new friend. He's the director of the video that I'm going to be in," LaCrae replied.

"Oh, so you got it? Congratulations," Julio said.

"Thank you," she replied.

"So what kind of video is it?" he asked.

"It's a rap video," LaCrae said.

"Oh," he said.

"What do you mean by that?" LaCrae asked, offended.

"Well, I mean… I thought you said you're going to be dancing. There's not much dancing in rap videos," Julio explained.

"There will be in this one. Q likes the way I dance and he thinks I will add something special to the video," LaCrae said.

"Something special? That's good. So, where's the video shoot?" Julio asked.

"In Brooklyn this Saturday," she informed him.

"Well then, I wish you good luck on your video. But you don't need it because, like your man Q said, you're already something special." Julio smiled at her. "You're really talented, LaCrae." Then he went down the steps and into his apartment.

LaCrae walked into the house to the sound of music playing in the living room. The woman singing had the sweetest, softest voice LaCrae had ever heard. The song was a mesmerizing love song and the dancer in her glided across the living room floor. It was one of those old-school jazz records. LaCrae looked over and saw Mae sitting in the chair next to the window with her feet up and her eyes closed. The music obviously affected her, too.

"Grandma?" LaCrae said quietly.

"Oh…hey. You're home," Mae said.

"Yes. Can I talk to you for a second?" LaCrae asked.

"Sure," Mae said and reached over to turn off the record player.

"Sorry to disturb you," LaCrae said.

"You're not," Mae replied.

"That was a nice song. Who is it?" LaCrae inquired. "I've never heard that song before."

"Well, that's because it's some girl from back in my day. She never became big and famous, so you will probably never hear her anywhere else but on my old record player," Mae explained.

"It was really pretty," LaCrae said.

"Yeah, it was. So, what do you want to talk to me about?" Mae asked.

"I just wanted to tell you that I went to an audition today and I got the part," LaCrae said. She didn't want to tell her grandmother that it was for a rap video because she didn't want the same response she got from Julio.

LaCrae waited for her grandmother to say something. But the words didn't come out quickly. Mae leaned back in the chair and turned her head from LaCrae. The silence made LaCrae nervous. What if her grandmother yelled at her like her mother did? Or told her she should get out of her house? Then what was she going to do?

"You know, the problem with life is that the moment we think we got it all figured out, something else pops up," Mae said as she looked out the window.

"I don't know what you mean," LaCrae said.

"Oh, just something that old people like me say," Mae replied. "If this is what you want, then I'm happy for you."

"You are?" LaCrae asked, skeptical of her grandmother's calm demeanor.

"Yes, I am," said Mae.

"Thank you, Grandma!" LaCrae jumped up and went over to give her a hug. "Oh! I'm going out with a friend tonight to celebrate."

"The same friend that brought you home in that big ol' fancy car?" Mae asked.

"Yes," LaCrae answered.

"Have fun." Mae turned back towards the window with sadness in her eyes.

LaCrae ran upstairs to her room to look for something to wear but her grandmother's words kept ringing in her ears. Her grandmother was so calm, as if she knew something that nobody else knew. She didn't yell or try to control LaCrae. She just said 'have fun.' This was not what LaCrae was used to. Fran would have tied her to the bed before letting her go out with some guy she didn't know. But not her grandmother. Nothing seemed surprising or alarming to her. She wasn't freaking out over the thought of LaCrae leaving the house late at night with a strange man. She just said to 'have fun.'

LaCrae sat on her bed for a moment and wondered where her grandmother's mind goes when she has that distant look in her eyes, or when her eyes are closed as though she's sleeping but she's actually wide awake. She wondered during those moments what it was that her grandmother saw and whom she was with.

Just then she heard that song playing again downstairs and LaCrae stood up and began to dance. She, too, closed her eyes and envisioned herself on a big stage in front of a crowd of people, all cheering for her and watching in amazement at the way her body moved. There was something about that music and the singer's voice that made LaCrae feel free and safe. That voice was calming and soothing, young and vibrant. It made her feel like the world was full of possibilities. That voice was also strangely familiar. LaCrae felt the singer knew all about her passion and dreams. They were connected. The voice sang a song of a love that LaCrae knew nothing about, but she danced to every melody, every word.

Sexy Enough

It took LaCrae hours to get ready. She decided to wear a tight, black dress that she'd brought with her. It was knee length but LaCrae cut it shorter so that it reached mid-thigh. She fixed her make-up and put on bright red lipstick. She wore her hair curlier than usual and slid her feet into a pair of heels she rarely wore. They were so high that she almost fell over when she tried to walk in them. Then she put on her favorite pair of silver hoop earrings and matching necklace.

After she was fully dressed, LaCrae took a look at herself in the mirror and hoped that Q and his friends would think she was sexy enough. While she admired herself in the mirror, she noticed, through the window, Q's truck pulling up outside. She took one final look at herself, grabbed her purse, and then ran down the stairs and out the door. After closing the front door she realized that she didn't even say goodbye to her grandmother. But LaCrae figured she was asleep anyway, so it didn't matter. Besides, she had already told her that she was going out.

From her bedroom, Mae could hear LaCrae moving about hastily and then the slamming of the front door. She got up and walked into LaCrae's room and looked through the window. She saw LaCrae looking far too grown for her age in a much too short dress. She watched as LaCrae ran to the waiting truck. When LaCrae opened the truck door, Mae could see a faint silhouette of a man with tattoos all up and down his arm. The sunglasses he wore blocked her from being able to view his face clearly. Mae was concerned. She wanted to yell out the window for LaCrae to get back inside the house. But she knew LaCrae was stubborn. The more you tell someone like that not to do something, the more determined they become to do it. She had tried the stern, heavy-handed parenting with Fran, but she didn't have the energy nor the strength to chase LaCrae down and knock some sense into her head. Mae walked back into her room and sat on her bed for a few minutes. Then she picked up the phone and began to dial.

"Hi, Ms. Mae," the voice on the other end answered.

"Julio, baby, did you just see LaCrae outside leaving?" Mae asked.

"Yes ma'am, I did," he answered.

Mae continued her line of questioning. "Do you know where she's going?"

"No ma'am, I don't," Julio replied.

"I know you're busy, baby, but if you can somehow find your way to see where she's headed I sho' would appreciate it," Mae said.

"I'm already following them, Ms. Mae," Julio said, smiling at the phone from the back of a taxi cab.

∗∗∗

Q kept glancing in LaCrae's direction, smiling slightly as he drove. LaCrae knew that he was pleased with the way she looked. He told her to make sure she was sexy and that's just what she did. His smile made her feel good.

"Not bad," Q finally said.

"Thanks," LaCrae replied, blushing.

"But if you're going to be rolling with me, you can't rock the fake stuff," he told her.

She didn't understand. "What do you mean?"

"Your jewelry's not right." Q reached over and opened the glove compartment with his free hand and pulled out diamond earrings and a long diamond necklace.

LaCrae had never seen anything so beautiful. She took off her own jewelry and put on the jewelry from Q. They matched perfectly with what she had on. The earrings made her hazel eyes sparkle and the necklace reached all the way down to her breasts, glistening against the smooth black fabric of her dress.

LaCrae turned to look at Q, giving him a big smile. "Thank you. They're perfect."

Q smiled back at her. He ran his fingers down her cheek, then laced them through her hair. The touch of Q's hand made LaCrae blush even more. She waited for him to say how beautiful she looked and that he was glad she was with him.

But instead, he said, "You should have worn your hair up."

✳✳✳

When they arrived at the club LaCrae got out of the truck and took Q by the hand. The line was long and LaCrae wondered how long it would take before they were able to get in. But Q pulled her by the hand, leading her up to the large doorman standing at the entrance of the club.

"What's good, Q?" asked the doorman.

"Nothing much man. What's it looking like in there?" Q replied.

"Yo, the hunnies are in the building, so you know the fellas are packed in there."

"No doubt," Q said while giving the doorman a hand-shake and a half hug.

Q grabbed hold of LaCrae's hand again and led her into the club. The music was loud and the place was jam-packed with people. The minute they walked in everyone started to stare. LaCrae felt special entering the club with Q because everyone knew him.

Q led LaCrae up a set of stairs and into an area that was guarded by large security men. There was food, lots of drinks, and girls with mini dresses dancing everywhere, even on the table tops. There were also several men, some of whom LaCrae recognized from the audition and others she'd seen on TV. LaCrae was nervous. She looked to Q to make her feel calm, but he was too preoccupied with greeting all the guys in the room to worry about her. LaCrae felt alone and out of her element. She sat on an empty sofa close to the bar and watched the party go on around her.

Everything seemed a little out of hand. The guys were clearly drunk and grabbing the girls, touching them everywhere. Something inside LaCrae told her that she needed to get out of there, but she had lost Q in the crowd of half-naked girls and intoxicated guys. LaCrae sat still with her heart beating a mile a minute. She hoped that no one would see her sitting there.

Suddenly, Q appeared and sat down next to her. "Why you sitting in the corner?"

"I don't know. You seemed busy. I didn't want to get in your way," she replied.

"Nah, you're not in my way," he said. "Look at all these hoes. You dance way better than them. You need to get up there and show them what you're made of," Q said, putting his arm around her.

"No. That's not my thing," she said, suddenly uncomfortable in his presence.

Q got up, went to the bar and poured a drink into a glass. He came back and sat down next to LaCrae, handing her the drink. "Here, take a sip of this."

LaCrae took the glass from him and took a little sip of it. The taste was so strong that she could barely get it down. It burned her throat and chest. She tried to hand the glass back to Q, shaking her head no. But Q refused to accept it. He went into the pocket of his pants and pulled out a bottle of pills. He took out a tiny pill and handed it to LaCrae.

"What's that?" she asked, scared to take it from him.

"Don't worry about it," Q answered. "It's just a muscle relaxer to help you loosen up a bit."

"No, I'm fine. I don't need anything," LaCrae said.

"Yeah, you do. You're starting to embarrass me. I told all these guys that you're the best dancer I know and you're sitting in the corner like a scared little girl. Now take this and get yourself out there." Q pushed the pill into LaCrae's hand.

LaCrae looked at Q and knew that he was not going to let up until she took the pill. Reluctantly, LaCrae put the pill in her mouth and swallowed. Q lifted her glass against her lips, sending the harsh drink down her throat. Then he got up to rejoin the party, leaving LaCrae behind on the couch. She sat there for a while and started to feel dizzy. There was ringing in her ears and the room began to move around her slowly.

Q returned and took her by the arm to pull her up from the sofa. He held her tightly around the waist and whispered in her ear, "You better not embarrass me." Then he yelled, "Yo, I got something right here!" He picked LaCrae up and forced her on top of the table, pushing off the girl who had been dancing on it.

LaCrae looked into Q's cold eyes as he silently dared her not to dance. Fearing what Q would do, LaCrae started to move. Pretty soon she heard the hooting and hollering of men as they pulled on her legs and smacked her butt. Someone even ran his hand between her thighs. LaCrae wanted so badly to get off that table as more hands pawed at her.

When she thought she just couldn't take it anymore, Q pulled her off, laughing. "Yo, no more freebies!" he announced to the crowd of men.

LaCrae tried to hold on to his hand, unsteady on her feet. But Q moved away from her, turning his attention to the next girl dancing on the table. LaCrae grabbed him and whispered in his ear, "Can we go, please?" Q moved away from her again.

LaCrae turned and realized that she was standing at the top of the stairs next to the entrance below. So she pushed her way through the big guys standing guard and stumbled her way down the stairs. She figured she would feel better if she could get to the bathroom and throw some water on her face. But the room was spinning and her vision was blurry. She could only hear the music playing and voices of strange men laughing and asking "Yo, baby. You alright?"

She continued to make her way through the crowd in hopes of finding the bathroom. Finally, LaCrae felt the wall and leaned her back against it. She couldn't move any more. Her legs and arms were not working and her vision was gone. Just as LaCrae started to slide down the wall, she felt a man's arm slide around her, picking her up and carrying her.

She didn't know who it was. She hoped that it was Q and he'd decided to take her home, but she couldn't tell who was carrying her. Panic set in. But there was nothing she could do. She had no control over her limbs to fight off the mystery man or to get down and run. As the cool, night air hit LaCrae's face, she was able to see just a little under a street light. Julio smiled down at her. He held her tighter and said "Everything's alright. I got you."

Growing Up To Do

A sunbeam peeked through the curtain, shining onto LaCrae's face. She covered her head with her pillow, trying to fall back asleep, but the throbbing in her head made that task difficult. Clutching her head in her hands, she hoped the pounding would stop. When that didn't work she tried rubbing her temples, gently at first, then more aggressively. She didn't understand why she had such a terrible headache.

Then she remembered what happened the night before. Some parts were hazy, like how she managed to leave the club and how she got into her bed. Did she dream about Julio carrying her, or had that actually happened? She remembered how safe she felt in his arms, how she trusted him to take care of her.

LaCrae tossed around in bed for a while, trying to figure out exactly what happened last night. Why did her head hurt so much when she barely had anything to drink? When lying in bed didn't improve her condition, she figured a hot shower would do the trick. She got out of bed and realized she was still wearing the dress she wore to the club. LaCrae peeled off the dress and stood under the shower. The hot water felt refreshing against her bare skin. For a moment her head felt normal again and the thumping seemed to have gone away. But after the shower, her cell phone rang, triggering the throbbing. LaCrae was pissed at the person on the other end until she picked up and realized it was Q.

"Hey, Ma," Q said when she answered the phone.

"Oh hey, Q. What's up?" LaCrae replied, unsure of what to say to him.

She still didn't know what happened to her or who brought her home. She didn't want to upset Q by asking the wrong question or seeming like she was accusing him of something. But she had so many questions.

"Where'd you disappear to?" Q asked.

"What do you mean?"

"I turned around and you were gone. My dude at the door said some Puerto Rican guy carried you out," Q said.

At that point LaCrae realized that it wasn't a dream. It was Julio who carried her. At least she had one of her questions answered. Now all she needed to know was why she felt so bad.

"Yeah, I wasn't feeling well," she explained. What did I have to drink?"

"I don't know. You just need to learn how to hold your liquor," Q told her.

"I guess," LaCrae said.

"I'm saying you can't just be leaving like that. You had my boys looking at me crazy," Q continued.

"I'm sorry. I didn't-"

"Don't even worry about it," he interrupted. "Just do better. Anyway, the video shoot's been moved up to tomorrow. Make sure you get there early."

"Alright. I'll...." The line went dead. Q hung up before LaCrae had the chance to tell him she was excited.

She thought Q was mad that she left him at the club and she felt guilty. After everything that he had done for her the last thing she wanted to do was to upset him. She wished Julio would have just left her alone or taken her back to Q.

LaCrae heard people talking as she made her way downstairs. It was Uncle Charlie and her grandmother. But their conversation was strange. They were arguing. She had never heard them argue before. LaCrae stopped at the top of the stairs and listened.

"Mama, you need to say something," Charlie said. "We all have to get ready."

"No and you're not going to say anything either, Charlie," Mae said.

"Mama, she needs to know. They all do," he said, trying to persuade her to change her mind.

"If you and Esther can't handle this, then let me know now," Mae replied.

"That's not what I'm saying, Mama. But we need to call Fran," Charlie insisted.

"No, no, no Charlie!" Mae yelled. "The last thing I need is to hear her mouth."

That was all LaCrae needed to hear. She knew they were talking about her. She was not going to let them ship her back to D.C. just because she went out and got drunk. She was so close to having everything she wanted.

LaCrae ran down the stairs and yelled, "I'm really sorry about last night. I promise it won't happen again."

Based on the look her grandmother and uncle exchanged, LaCrae realized they were not talking about her.

"What happened last night?" Charlie asked.

"I went out and got...well I mean...nothing really happened. Sorry," LaCrae said, feeling a bit embarrassed.

Charlie, puzzled by her outburst, asked, "Are you sure?"

"Yeah. I'm going to be on the porch," LaCrae said and made her way out the front door as quickly as she could.

✳✳✳

Once LaCrae was outside Charlie looked at Mae with a peculiar expression. "What's all that about?" he asked.

"That child got herself in all kinds of mess," Mae answered.

"What kind of mess?" he asked.

"The hell if I know," Mae said, shaking her head in disapproval. "She went out with some strange man in a big ol' fancy car. Julio had to bring her home last night, passed out."

Charlie was concerned about his niece. His concern heightened when he noticed his mother had that faraway look in her eyes. He knew what that look meant. He knew where she was and what she was thinking. It wasn't a happy place; it was a place of fear and panic. A place that not many people knew about. A few years after he married Esther he told her about that place, but his mother wasn't aware that Esther knew. For all Mae knew, her place was her quiet secret and she preferred it that way.

Charlie reached across the kitchen table and grabbed his mother's hand. Her son's touch brought Mae's mind back to the present. She glanced at him, smiled and patted his hand.

"I'll talk to her, Mama. She's going to be alright," Charlie said, giving his mother a wink and returning her smile.

✳✳✳

LaCrae sat on the steps and wondered what they were arguing about if it wasn't about her. What did her mother need to know? What did they all need to know? LaCrae tried to listen through the half-opened window, but the outside noise drowned out their voices. She knew something was definitely going on. It had to be important for her grandmother to be upset at the thought of others finding out. The urgency in her uncle's voice scared her. She wished she could hear something, just a bit more of what they were saying to help her solve the mystery.

"You know, you shouldn't be eavesdropping on other people's conversation,'" a voice said from behind her. LaCrae turned around to see Julio standing at the bottom of the stairs.

"I'm not eavesdropping. I was just wondering what they were talking about," LaCrae replied.

"That's called eavesdropping," Julio said, smiling as he came up the stairs and sat down next to her.

"Whatever," she said, pushing herself away from him. She was still upset that he brought her home the night before, making Q think she had left him. Q was pissed at her and it was all Julio's fault.

"Did I do something wrong...again?" Julio asked.

"Yes. You made Q mad at me!"

"What! He's mad at you? Wow!" Julio chuckled in disbelief.

"Why does everything amuse you? Yes, he's mad at me. I did leave without telling him anything.
He must have been worried that something happened to me."

"Oh please," Julio said, disgusted. "The only thing he was worried about was that he had to find a new girl to put on display for his boys."

"That was not what he was doing," she said.

"Are you serious?! I watched the whole thing go down. I saw you on top of that table, looking uncomfortable while those guys groped you. I saw your dude, Q, not giving a damn. I saw you falling down the stairs and damn near passing out in the middle of the club. Where was your man's concern for you then?"

LaCrae continued defending Q. "He was concerned! He just called me this morning to find out what happened to me!"

"He just called this morning? That's crazy," Julio said, chuckling again.

"What's crazy about that?" LaCrae asked.

"It's crazy that you don't even know how messed up you were. Do you realize that anything could have happened to you last night?"

LaCrae was angry. "I was fine. Q would have taken care of me."

"Q would have taken care of you? Right." Julio got up and headed down the stairs. He stopped at the bottom and turned back to LaCrae. "You know, you walk around here with this big chip on your shoulder acting like no one gets you. But the truth is they know you're a spoiled little girl who has a lot of growing up to do. The world is not about you, LaCrae. There are people and things out here that you're not prepared to deal with. You've got a lot of growing up to do."

Julio walked down to his apartment, leaving LaCrae sitting on the steps questioning everything that she'd come to know about herself. She had been so sure that she had everything figured out, but maybe Julio was right. Maybe there were things in life that she did not understand. Maybe she did have some growing up to do.

Julio's words echoed through LaCrae's head as she continued to sit on the stairs. The thought of Q being a horrible person was unbelievable to her. He'd been nothing but nice ever since the first time they met. He was the only one who believed in her and was actually trying to help her.

LaCrae wondered how someone who took that much interest in her could be the sort of person Julio was making him out to be. She leaned her shoulder against the railing and stared up at the sky.

She felt a tug on her left shoulder as Charlie sat down beside her.

"How are you doing, sweetheart?" he asked, his eyes searching her face.

"I'm doing ok," LaCrae replied.

"Are you sure?" he asked. "New York isn't an easy place to navigate, especially for a young girl."

"Uncle Charlie, I'm 19."

"Yeah, you are. But you're also going to clubs and getting drunk at 19," he said. "Which tells me that perhaps you need a little more guidance than you realize."

"See, I knew you guys were talking about me," she said, turning away in frustration.

"Relax. I told you we were not talking about you," he said, grabbing her hand.

"Then what were you guys talking about?" LaCrae asked again, locking eyes with him.

"Nothing for you to worry about right now," he said, letting her hand go and looking off into the distance. LaCrae could tell he wanted to say more but he didn't know how. Then he quickly turned back to her, mentally shaking off whatever thoughts were running through his head. "Anyway, I just wanted to talk to you because your grandmother is a little concerned about some of the choices she sees you making."

"What choices?" LaCrae asked.

"I don't know. Maybe like the one you made last night?" he replied.

"Grandma doesn't understand."

"Don't be so sure about that. Your grandma may surprise you," he said with a smile. "Anyway, just be careful and if you need anything or if you're not sure of something, I'm always here."

"Ok." LaCrae smiled at her uncle, leaning in as he pulled her close for a hug.

Charlie got up and walked to his car. After watching him drive off, LaCrae headed into the house.

Ain't No Good

Julio sat on his sofa with the TV on but had no clue what he was watching. He was restless and agitated. He wanted to go back outside and apologize to LaCrae, not so much for what he said but for the way he said it. He didn't mean to lose it on her the way he did, but he wanted to get through to her. He hated that she was upset with him, especially since the person she should be upset with is Q.

Although Julio didn't know Q personally, something about him didn't feel right. Julio had known a lot of guys like Q, especially the one that got his sister strung out. Guys like Q preyed on young girls and made them do things that they wouldn't ordinarily do. They made girls give up all their power and made them believe that they were worth nothing. Julio felt he was watching what happened to his sister unfold all over again, but this time, LaCrae was the victim. He'd promised Mae that he would look out for LaCrae and that's what he intended on doing. Besides, he felt a strange pull to LaCrae. Something about her made him smile like a school girl whenever she came around. The way she acted toughed amused him. He couldn't rationalize his feelings. He just wanted to protect her and keep her safe.

Julio got out his laptop and began to search for anything he could find on Q. From what he found online, Q was the real deal. He had directed multiple music videos and seemed to know all the big wigs in the music industry, or, at the very least, was close enough to take a picture with them. But there was still something about Q that felt wrong. Julio grabbed his cell and reluctantly called the only person who may know more information.

"Hey, papi. I knew you couldn't stay away," cooed the female voice on the other end.

Julio cringed. "Hey, Sonya."

Sonya was gorgeous but far from Julio's type. She was the kind of girl who always wanted attention. Her life goals were to wear the most expensive clothes, drive the best cars, and wear the flashiest jewelry. There was no real substance to her. They couldn't even have a full conversation without her asking if he could buy her something. But Sonya did know the streets. She had even been in a few music videos and hung around a lot of music artists. If anyone would know about Q, it would be her.

"What's up, papi?"

"I was wondering if you could tell me what you know about this guy."

"What guy?" Sonya asked.

"He goes by Q and he's some kind of music video director," Julio explained.

"Hell yeah, I know Q!" she exclaimed. "Why you asking, papi?"

"I'm just trying to find out what his deal is," Julio said.

Sonya snickered and mumbled. "Please."

"What's that about?" Julio asked.

"Don't think don't nobody know that your girl been running around here with Q. He been talking about how he's going to make her the next big video vixen. She ain't even that cute," Sonya said with an attitude.

"Watch it," Julio warned.

"No, she needs to watch it."

"Why?"

"Because Q ain't no good," Sonya said.

"What do you mean by that?" Julio asked, alarmed.

"Let's just say he keeps his girls in check like most pimps do. That's all I'm saying," Sonya replied.

Julio was quiet. He knew there was something off about this dude. His instincts were right. Q was no good and LaCrae was in trouble. He wanted to hang the phone up in Sonya's ear and run to tell LaCrae what he'd learned about Q, but Sonya kept going on about how she wanted to go out with Julio. She was trying her best to get his attention but he could only think of LaCrae. Finally, Sonya got angry and said "If you ain't going to listen to me then I'm hanging up."

Julio barely said bye before making his way to the door. But by the time he got outside he could see LaCrae halfway down the street in her dance clothes.

LaCrae had grown tired of sitting around the house, staring out the window. She'd called Q but he didn't pick up. She sent him a text message that said: *"I'm really sorry*

for last night. I hope you're not angry with me." But again, he didn't respond. Finally, LaCrae put on her dance clothes and headed to the community center. As she left the house she heard Julio opening his door. She hurried down the street to avoid having to deal with him.

When she entered the center she saw Domonique talking to a group of people. LaCrae did her best to avoid eye contact with her. Domonique just didn't know when to quit and, much like Julio, LaCrae didn't want to deal with her. Before LaCrae could make it safely out of sight she heard Domonique call out, "LaCrae! LaCrae!"

She turned around, visibly irritated. She wanted Domonique to know how annoying she was becoming and that it was time for her to stop. But LaCrae's aggravated expression did not deter Domonique. She ran up to LaCrae with a woman LaCrae had never seen before.

"Hey," Domonique said almost out of breath. "I'm so glad you came in today. I want you to meet someone."

"I'm really in a rush. I want to get a practice in before you close," LaCrae said.

"It will only take a second," Domonique insisted. "This is Mrs. Davis from the Dance Academy. I was just telling her about you."

LaCrae looked at the skinny, tall, black woman standing next to Domonique. She looked regal. Her facial expression was impassive as she looked LaCrae over. But LaCrae was not intimidated. She looked at the woman and said, "Hello."

The woman nodded her head as she and LaCrae stared at one another. LaCrae didn't know what Mrs. Davis wanted her to do, but she had no time or patience for a stare down.

"Ok, well nice to meet you. I have to go," LaCrae finally said as she turned and walked away.

Once LaCrae was out of sight Mrs. Davis turned to Domonique. "That's the phenomenon you wanted me to meet? She seems like your average, unmannered teenager to me."

"I know, Louise, but just go and watch her. I promise you'll be blown away," Domonique said.

"I don't know, Dom, I have other things I could be doing with my time."

"Just trust me," Domonique said. Mrs. Davis agreed and walked over with Domonique to the room where LaCrae practiced.

LaCrae was completely unaware she was being watched. She finished stretching and then turned on the music. The thumping of the hip-hop beat took over her body. She did steps she'd seen on TV and some of her own original moves. She flipped and leaped across the floor. Her arms and legs were moving fast and catching every beat. Pretty soon sweat started to drip down her face, but LaCrae did not stop. She was in her zone and nothing could break her concentration.

Mrs. Davis' face remained expressionless as she watched LaCrae. Finally, she turned to Domonique. "I've seen enough," she said and started to walk away.

Domonique chased after her. "Wait, what did you think?"

Mrs. Davis said nothing more, giving Domonique an over the shoulder wave goodbye. Domonique looked back at the room where LaCrae practiced. She knew LaCrae had something special and could not believe Mrs. Davis didn't see it. She took off after her again. "Did you really not just see what I saw?!"

Mrs. Davis stopped walking and turned to Domonique. "She is incredible. Exactly what we're looking for. But does she want it?"

"Of course she does, Louise," Domonique declared.

"It doesn't look that way to me, Dom. I've got girls at the academy that would cut their right arm off to have me watch them dance for one second. I'll tell you what - if you can convince her to audition, I'll hold a spot for her," Mrs. Davis offered. She walked away leaving Domonique behind to contemplate how she was going to get LaCrae to the audition.

✳✳✳

When the music stopped LaCrae sat down against the wall to catch her breath. So many things were running through her mind that she could hardly keep them straight. What Julio said really bothered her. It didn't make her mad, it just hurt her feelings. For him to say that she needed to grow up and that she didn't know anything about life was simply not true. She knew enough about life to know who she was and what she wanted. He knew nothing about her, and he sure didn't have the right to talk to her the way he did.

LaCrae was just about to start practicing again when her phone rang. She lit up when she saw that it was Q.

"Hey!" she answered.

"What's up, ma?"

LaCrae couldn't tell by his voice whether he was still upset with her. She held her breath and waited for him to tell her that he no longer wanted her to be in the video. That he had changed his mind about helping her.

"You home?" Q asked.

"No," she said, "I'm at the community center down the street."

"Meet me outside in 5 minutes," he demanded.

"I'm all sweaty. I've been dancing. Can I go home and get cleaned up first?" LaCrae asked.

"Nah, ma. A little sweat don't bother me."

"Ok, then I'm on my way outside," LaCrae said just before he hung up.

She hurried to the ladies restroom to fix herself up. She remembered how Q stressed that she look good the night they went to the club. She didn't want to upset him again, especially when he was giving her another shot at proving herself to him. She was not going to fail him this time.

LaCrae made sure her hair was perfectly pulled up, the curls hanging in a ponytail. She used paper towels to wipe the sweat from her forehead and underarms. She checked her watch and ran out of the bathroom. She didn't even realize Domonique was trying to get her attention.

Q pulled up in his Escalade just as LaCrae made it outside. Every girl around was practically drooling over Q's ride. LaCrae chuckled to herself at the look on their faces as their jaws dropped when she opened the passenger door and got in. Q was the man, and LaCrae felt special being with him.

"Hi." LaCrae searched his face to see if he was mad at her.

"What's up, ma?" Q said, barely looking at her as he drove down the street.

She wanted to ask where they were going, but his silence made her nervous. She looked out the window and tried to get an idea of where they were headed, but it was pointless. She didn't know enough about New York.

Finally, he parked in front of a brick building that had no signs of what it is used for. Q got out and started walking towards the front door. LaCrae quickly followed behind him. Once inside the building they walked down a hallway that led to a single door. On the other side of the door was an office waiting area. The waiting area was nearly empty except for a girl sitting behind a receptionist desk. The girl barely looked up to acknowledge their arrival.

"Yo, I'll be in my office if you need me," Q said to the receptionist.

"Ok," she said, finally lifting her head to look directly at LaCrae. She stared at LaCrae as she followed Q into the office. LaCrae felt as though the girl was trying to silently communicate to her. Suddenly she felt uneasy. She could hear Julio's voice in her head, telling her not to trust Q. Her instincts told her she shouldn't be in Q's office, at least not alone.

Q sat on the sofa against the wall and stared at LaCrae. She looked around the office nervously. The room was filled with awkward silence until she finally worked up the nerve to ask, "What are we doing here?"

"I thought you would want to see my spot,” Q replied. "This is where I do my business. Come over here and sit next to me." He patted the sofa.

LaCrae slowly walked over to the couch but sat down on the opposite end. Q laughed and moved closer, putting his arm around her shoulders. His touch turned her nervousness into fear. With his free hand, he slowly began to stroke her stomach and made his way up to her breasts. LaCrae was frozen in place. She found Q attractive but she just wasn't ready for all of this. She tried to gently wiggle herself free, but that only seemed to urge him on even more. He kissed her neck and tightened his grip around her.

"Wait, Q.” LaCrae grabbed his shoulder and tried to push him off. He didn't budge.

"Relax, ma.” He pushed her further down onto the sofa and climbed on top of her.
LaCrae's pulse was racing.

"Q, stop!" she yelled.

But he was too strong. He pulled at her clothes. Tears filled her eyes, her heart pounded in her chest. She was terrified.

"Please stop! STOP!" LaCrae yelled.

Q lifted his head and gripped her jaw. LaCrae stared into his cold eyes through her tears. Suddenly, he let her go and got up. LaCrae curled up against the arm of the sofa and cried hysterically.

"So what? We going to play some little kid shit?" Q asked.

But LaCrae was too terrified to respond or even look at him. This wasn't the guy she'd met in D.C., the one who believed in her. The one who thought she was talented and said she was going to be great.

"Yo, ma, calm down. I misread the signs. I thought we were on the same page. I'm sorry, aight?" Q crouched down in front of her, placing a hand on her knee.

That was the guy LaCrae knew. The gentle voice and touch. Though she was shaking uncontrollably, she tried her best to gather herself. Maybe she had given Q the wrong impression.

"Look at me," Q said, lifting her head. "You need to be clear about what you want."

LaCrae nodded as she wiped the tears from her eyes. She was terrified of Q, but she believed that everything that happened was her fault.

He stood. "Get your shit. Let's go."

As they walked out of the office LaCrae noticed that the girl behind the desk was gone. She was completely alone in the building with Q. LaCrae wrapped her arms around herself and walked quickly down the hallway and out the door. The cool, night air washed over her face and dried most of her tears. She nearly jumped out of her skin when the keyless entry chirped to unlock the doors.

The drive to her grandmother's house seemed long. LaCrae leaned against the door, holding herself and trying not to cry again. When the truck finally came to a stop, Q reached over and squeezed LaCrae's arm so tight she was positive there would be a bruise.

"I'm not going to put up with this little kid shit for much longer. You hear me?"

LaCrae nodded. "I'm sorry."

She didn't want to make Q angrier. All she wanted was to get out of that truck. She looked out the window wishing Julio was somewhere around, but for the first time, he was nowhere in sight. LaCrae held her breath, waiting for Q to let go of her arm and fighting back her tears.

"Make sure you have your ass at the shoot on time. I'm not coming to get you. Maybe if you start walking you'll start appreciating some shit." He let go of her arm.

LaCrae opened the door and jumped out. She ran up the steps to the brownstone as Q sped away. She hurried through the front door and up the stairs until she was safely in her bedroom with the door locked behind her. She slid down the wall, wanting to scream, but there was a soft tapping at the door.

"LaCrae, baby. Are you ok?" Mae asked from the other side of the door.

"Yeah, Grandma, I'm fine," LaCrae replied, trying to hide the terror in her voice.

She knew her grandmother would never understand what she just went through. She didn't want to hear anyone else say "I told you so." LaCrae curled up on the bedroom floor, clutching her knees to her chest. She wished the day would end and she could wake up in the morning like nothing ever happened.

Life Has a Way of Replaying

LaCrae woke up the next morning unable to forget what happened the day before. It was running through her mind like a bad movie scene permanently stuck on a loop. Q had scared her worse than anybody ever had and she didn't know how to deal with him now. Should she still let him help her with her dance career? Should she just walk away and never call him again? Could she accept what happened as a one-time thing and that he would never do anything like that again?

She couldn't think straight. Nothing made sense anymore. She had trusted Q to take care of her. She'd always been a good judge of character, but she felt she was so off about Q. She thought he was the answer to her prayers but now she seemed to be living a nightmare. She had dropped out of school, left home, and practically disowned her mother all because of the promises Q made her. Now she had nothing.

LaCrae picked up her phone to plug it into the charger and noticed she had a text message from Q. She hesitated to open it, suspecting he had texted to tell her not to go to the video shoot. Her finger quivered when it tapped on the message.

"Hey ma, yo sorry for the misunderstanding. You were sending out those signals and you sexy as hell. But it's all good ma. We good. See you later at the shoot. Yo, bring that jewelry I gave you.

To LaCrae, he sounded like the man she'd met in D.C. Maybe she had sent out the wrong signals and made him think that she wanted to go further. She was comforted by the fact that Q took the time to apologize. She started to get ready for the video shoot.

✳✳✳

LaCrae stood at the bottom of the brownstone's steps. She was too afraid to move. The thought of seeing Q so soon after what happened sent cold shivers down her spine. Part of her had accepted his apology, but part of her was still in panic mode. She was once again consumed by fear. Images of the day before flooded her mind, so vivid that she could feel Q's hands holding her down and groping her. She stood on the sidewalk gasping for air.

The hand on her shoulder made her flinch so hard that she almost lost her balance. Julio's startled face brought a bit of comfort to LaCrae. He was familiar. His presence made her feel safe and her anxiety slowly began to dwindle away.

"LaCrae, I'm sorry. I didn't mean to scare you." His eyes searched hers for clues as to why she was so afraid. Julio's gut feeling was that something had happened between LaCrae and Q, but LaCrae didn't say anything. He wanted to check her body from head to toe to see if she was hurt but he knew she would never allow that. Although LaCrae was strong willed, Julio knew that she couldn't handle a guy like Q. Julio wanted to protect her. He wanted to hold her in his arms and never let her go. He wanted to make it so Q and any other guy like him could never get to her.

"Oh...no...you didn't scare me. I just wasn't expecting anyone to come by, that's all," LaCrae said stumbling over her words.

"You didn't expect anyone to come by? You're standing on the sidewalk, LaCrae. People are going to come by," Julio pointed out. "What's wrong?"

"Nothing's wrong. I just…nothing's wrong," LaCrae replied, unable to think of a lie.

"Are you sure? Because you could tell me any-"

"I said nothing's wrong," LaCrae snapped. "I have to get to my video shoot."

"Ok. Would you like some company? I would love to see a real life video shoot." Julio was lying. He just wanted to stay close to LaCrae to make sure she was alright and that Q stayed far away from her.

"Um…if you want to I guess that's ok." She was relieved. She'd had her doubts about Julio, but her grandmother and uncle trusted him. She figured she should as well. Besides, Julio had done nothing to hurt her. In fact, he'd always tried to help her.

LaCrae's face softened. She truly saw Julio for the first time. He noticed. The way she looked at him silently conveyed her gratitude. He noticed that, too. Julio knew something bad had happened, but it was up to LaCrae to tell him what that something was. Until then, he planned on staying close to her.

The two of them made their way down the street towards the subway. Everything around them seemed calm and peaceful. As far as LaCrae was concerned, they could have continued their walk forever. Julio's voice drove out the image of Q's actions the day before. She no longer shivered with fear. The terror that had settled in the pit of her stomach vanished and was replaced by the joy she felt hearing the sound of her own laughter as Julio told not-so-funny jokes. For a moment, nothing else mattered.

✳✳✳

When they arrived at the video shoot the sight of the crowd was overwhelming. LaCrae looked around at faces filled with desperation, longing to be a part of the phenomenon that was about to take place. LaCrae crossed her arms, hugging herself as she and Julio weaved through the crowd. Her eyes landed on Q. A chill ran down her spine. She stopped walking, no longer able to move. Then she felt Julio's hand on hers.

"It's ok," he whispered.

LaCrae took her eyes off Q and turned towards Julio. The look in his light brown eyes felt like a warm embrace. She was safe with him. The voice that called out to her broke the moment of serenity.

"Yo, ma! You're almost late," Q said. But she didn't look his way. She kept her eyes glued on Julio and held on tight to his hand. She wanted to tell him to get her out of there but she couldn't form the words.

Q walked up to her and grabbed her arm. Julio turned to Q, pulling LaCrae out of his grip.

"Yo, ma, I don't have time for this. You still doing this or what?" Q said, throwing a nasty look at Julio.

"Um…yeah…I'm still doing this," LaCrae replied.

"Ok. Then come on," Q said, pulling LaCrae behind him.

Both men kept their eyes locked on each other until Q and LaCrae disappeared into the crowd. Q pulled LaCrae behind him as they walked towards a white trailer with dark tinted windows. Inside there were a few scantily clad girls sitting on top of a wooden table and folding chairs. Q yelled at them to get out and they hurried outside without a sound. LaCrae watched as Q slammed the door behind them and then turned to her.

"You just love to embarrass me, don't you?!" he yelled.

"No, I don't," LaCrae replied, her voice quivering. Q stared at her, the cold look from the day before returned to his face. She was terrified. She wanted to run and hide, but Q was blocking the only way out.

"Yeah, you do." He stalked towards her. "How the hell you think that makes me look when my girl brings some fucking dude with her?"

"I'm sorry…I didn't mean to," LaCrae apologized as tears fell from her eyes.

"You're always fucking sorry!" Q yelled. "Where's the shit I gave you?"

Her hands shaking, LaCrae reached into her bag and pulled out the earrings and necklace Q gave her. She slowly handed the entangled jewelry over to him. The sight of it infuriated him even more.

"Do you know how expensive this shit was?!" He reared back and threw the jewelry against the wall.

"What…what did I do?" LaCrae said, crying hysterically.

"Stop crying all the damn time!" He picked up one of the folding chairs and flung it across the trailer.

LaCrae screamed and covered her ears, trying to block out the sound of the chair crashing into the wall and splintering into pieces. Q ran towards her, grabbed her by the shoulders and slammed her against the wall.

The trailer door flung open. Julio ran in and jerked Q by the collar of his shirt. He dragged Q off of LaCrae and pinned him against the wall. Julio was furious. He wanted to put his fist through Q's face.

The two men stood eye to eye, hands gripped around each other's collars. LaCrae yelled for Julio to leave with her, but he didn't move. His eyes were fixed on Q. In Q he saw the man who got his sister hooked on drugs and then pimped her out. He saw all the men who came in and out of his mother's life, interfering with her ability to be a good mother to him and his siblings. Q was the enemy. He was the evil that needed to be destroyed before another young girl ended up dead like his sister. But before Julio could act, a group of security guards came in and pulled the two men apart. LaCrae grabbed Julio's arm, tugging him out of the trailer.

"You're done!" Q screamed after them. "You hear me, bitch! You're done!"

✳✳✳

They had left the video shoot, but Julio's anger continued to surge. He wanted to go back and finish what he started with Q. But the sight of LaCrae on the subway bench, head in hands and sobbing uncontrollably, made him realize that she needed him to be there for her. Julio sat down beside her, wrapping her in his arms. They sat there for a moment in silence as LaCrae wept.

"Everyone was right," LaCrae said, lifting her head from Julio's shoulder and wiping the tears from her eyes. "I'm so stupid."

"Don't be hard on yourself," Julio said. "Guys like that prey on girls like you."

She sighed. "You mean stupid girls like me."

"No," Julio answered with a smile. "I mean talented girls with big dreams."

"Well, I'm not going to do this ever again," she declared. "I'm packing my bags and heading back to D.C. as soon as I can."

"Wait!" Julio said, suddenly alarmed. "You can't do that."

"Why not?" LaCrae asked.

"Because you can't. You have to stick around for a while," he insisted.

"Look, Julio, I know that maybe we could have…you know. But I just need to get home," LaCrae said, trying to let him down easily.

"No, it's not that, LaCrae," Julio said, his eyes intense. "Look, I'm not supposed to say anything, but it's your grandmother."

"What about my grandmother?" LaCrae asked.

"She's sick, LaCrae," Julio confessed. "She has cancer and she doesn't have much longer to live."

"What? That's not true." LaCrae couldn't believe it. Her grandmother looked perfectly healthy. She hadn't seen any signs of her being sick or anything out of character.

Then it hit her. The image of the wig and her grandmother's missing hair filled her mind.

"It's true, LaCrae, and she needs you to be around at least for a little while longer. She may not say anything but I know she likes having you around," Julio said.

LaCrae remembered the conversation she walked in on between her uncle and grandmother. She realized now that they were discussing her grandmother's illness and her uncle was trying to convince her to tell the rest of the family before it was too late. Her grandmother was dying and she'd been so busy following Q around and falling for his lies that she hadn't taken the time to notice. LaCrae hadn't spent any time with her or taken care of her. She was angry at herself for being so oblivious to what really mattered. She vowed then and there that things were going to change.

✳✳✳

LaCrae walked into the house, her clothes still disheveled from her fight with Q and her cheeks stained with remnants of her tears. All she wanted to do was run to her grandmother and give her a hug. Tell her that she knew and that she was here for her. Just as LaCrae was about to call out for her, Mae came out of the kitchen. She was startled by LaCrae's appearance. LaCrae immediately ran her fingers through her hair and tried to fix herself up.

Mae ran to LaCrae, pulling her into a loving embrace. "Oh my Lord, child! What in the world happened to you?"

"I'm fine, Grandma. Really, I am. It looks bad but I really am fine," LaCrae reassured her.

"What kind of video shoot did you go to where you come out looking like someone been tossing you around like a ragdoll?" Mae asked.

"Grandma, it's nothing, I swear," LaCrae insisted.

"No, it's not nothing," Mae said. "I knew you shouldn't have gone to that place, I just knew it."

"Grandma, please don't worry. It's nothing," LaCrae said, trying to calm her down.

"I need to call your uncle. He'd know how to handle this." Mae released LaCrae and reached for the house phone.

"No, Grandma, please don't call Uncle Charlie," LaCrae pleaded.

"Then I'm calling the police."

"No, Grandma, don't!"

"Child, if you don't start explaining then I'm going to have to call your Mama, and Lord knows I don't want to hear Fran's mouth today," Mae said.

LaCrae sat down on the sofa and Mae sat down next to her. LaCrae told her every single detail of what happened, starting from meeting Q in D.C. all the way through how she ended up looking the way she currently looked. She even told her about the day before when Q attacked her in his office. When LaCrae finished explaining she thought for sure her grandmother would be upset. She prepared herself for the phone call that would surely be made to her mother. But that didn't happen.

Mae got up, walked over to her collection of music and pulled out an album. She placed it on the old turntable and then sat in the recliner next to it. The song that began to play was the one she played countless times before. The one LaCrae couldn't help but to dance to in her room. The one that spoke to LaCrae like nothing else had before.

"Grandma," LaCrae said softly, "are you mad at me?"

"No, child," Mae said. "I can't say that I'm mad."

"Then what is it?" LaCrae asked.

"It's just sometimes life has a way of replaying itself," Mae explained.

LaCrae didn't understand. "What do you mean?"

"I mean it's time we had a conversation," Mae said, reaching over to turn off the turntable and gazing intensely into LaCrae's eyes.

PART II

Uncle Buck

Growing up in small town North Carolina was no picnic, especially in 1960. A bunch of them college kids from up there in Greensboro had just caused some commotion about a sit-in or something crazy like that. And boy, were those white folks mad at every black person they came across because of it. We lived in a small town with nothing but fields and dirt roads. We black folks lived on one side of the train tracks and the white folks lived on the other. All of us who lived there stayed there. There really wasn't a need to go anyplace else. Old man Jenkins had a convenience store that sold everything from hair grease to pork loins. The white mailman dropped the black folks' mail off to Mr. Jones, who saw to it that everyone got their mail. All the kids went to the same school and everyone knew each other. Lord, it was such a boring town.

It was the worst feeling in the world to know that when you woke up every day you'd be doing the same thing, going to the same places, and seeing the same people. It was as though I had lived the same day over and over for the last eighteen years. I hated it.

My only saving grace was the church, which, by the way, everyone attended. Yes, Mt. Zion of the Redeemer Baptist Church was my special place. But only because it was the only place where people could hear me sing. Oh, how I loved to sing. I would sing in the shower, in the mirror, while I was cooking, and anywhere else. But the church is where I had an audience. People told me that when I sing, it sounds like I've been touched by the Holy Spirit. They didn't know that the only thing I saw when I closed my eyes during a song was me on some big-time stage with cameras pointed in my direction. During those moments on that church altar, I was a star. Then my eyes would open and there I was, right back in that small town looking at the same people, reliving the same day.

I needed a change and that change came when Uncle Buck rolled back into town. Uncle Buck was my Mama's little brother. His daughter, Vivian, was my favorite cousin. Vivian was a bit older than me and she had found her way to New York City. Man, I idolized Vivian. She'd done something I only dreamt of. Vivian wrote me a letter almost every day telling me all the things she was doing, all the places she went to, and all the people she met. Vivian was living the life.

Now, people would say Uncle Buck was one of those hoodlums, the ones who couldn't seem to stay on the right side of the law. But I loved him just as much as I loved his daughter, and seeing him meant the world to me.

We walked out of the church doors one Sunday afternoon, and there was Uncle Buck dressed in a powder blue suit with matching shoes and hat. He stood next to his 1957 red Chevy that had a silver line that ran down the sides. It looked like a bullet, even though I'd never seen a bullet in person, but if I had, I imagined that's what it would look like.

When Mama saw Uncle Buck she took off running and gave him a big hug. Mama always greeted Uncle Buck like that. She said that seeing Uncle Buck lets her know that he's still alive somewhere in the world. I guess Mama always expected to hear news of Uncle Buck's death, but he always came home.

"Come here, Lil Bit," Uncle Buck said as he scooped me up into a hug.

Uncle Buck wasn't a big man. He was tall and skinny, yet he always seemed so strong. Something about him made everyone around him feel at ease. He could make you smile with just his smile alone and he made you feel special as though you're the only person on the planet. Mama called it his charm.

"Put her down, Buck. She's too old for you to be lifting like that," Mama said to Uncle Buck.

"She is not. Mae you 'bout eight, nine?" Uncle Buck asked as he looked me up and down.

"I just turned eighteen, Uncle Buck," I replied with a chuckle.

"That's right, Buck. You haven't been around in a while to see her grow. But we're going to leave all that alone until later. Come on, let's go get you something to eat," Mama said, giving him a stern look.

Uncle Buck winked at me and whispered, "Looks like I'm in trouble, Lil Bit." We both laughed as we all got into his car and headed down the dirt road to my house.

Mama and I were so excited to see Uncle Buck that we forgot Daddy and my siblings, Curtis Jr. and Francine, or Buddy and Franny for short, were waiting at the house.

My siblings were much younger than me. Buddy was ten and Franny was eight. They didn't really know Uncle Buck like I did. But Daddy knew him all too well and he was never one of Uncle Buck's biggest fans. Daddy thought Uncle Buck was a bad influence to have around his kids. He barely wanted Uncle Buck around Mama.

Daddy thought one day Uncle Buck would bring trouble to our front door and Daddy didn't want any trouble from anybody. He was a proud man and liked things around him to be peaceful and quiet. Uncle Buck and Daddy were the exact opposite. If Daddy came across a white man, he'd say 'Yes, Sir', but Uncle Buck would look that white man in the eye and dare him to do something. Daddy hated that about Uncle Buck.

"Why tempt the white man?" Daddy would ask. "You know he don't like niggers."

"That's just it, Curtis. We ain't niggers. And I'ma keep tempting the white man until he sees me as his equal and not a nigger," Uncle Buck would reply.

The two of them would go on for hours about that same subject and neither one of them would care to listen to the other.

As we rode down the dirt road leading to my house I could see Daddy sitting on the porch. Uncle Buck chuckled to himself at the sight of Daddy. Mama looked nervous as she looked back at me.

"Now, Buck, don't you get him started," Mama warned.

"I won't, sis," he said, still chuckling.

I shook my head to myself knowing that Uncle Buck couldn't resist pushing Daddy's buttons. It was like he took pleasure in hearing Daddy yell at him. Mama always said that the two of them were like oil and water. But Daddy said he just doesn't trust Uncle Buck as far as he could throw him.

The car barely stopped before Mama jumped out and ran up to Daddy. He frowned when he saw Uncle Buck step out of the fancy car.

"Curtis, ain't it great Buck came for a visit?" Mama asked Daddy.

"He's probably hiding or on the run." Daddy stared down Uncle Buck.

"Oh, big brother Curtis, now you know I don't run from nothing, baby," Uncle Buck said with his arms stretched out wide and a big grin on his face.

"That means you hiding from someone. What you do, piss off one of those white boys up North?" Daddy asked.

"Now you know I don't hide from no white man. I'll leave that to the rest of you scared niggers." Uncle Buck laughed and propped his foot on the bumper of his car.

"Buck!" Mama yelled as she held Daddy back from jumping off the porch.

"Oh, it's just a joke, sis." Uncle Buck walked over to Daddy and give him a hug. Daddy didn't hug him back. Instead, he pulled away and turned to walk into the house as Uncle Buck stood there and howled with laughter.

Mama smacked Uncle Buck on his arm. "I told you not to mess with him," she scolded.

Uncle Buck, still laughing, tickled me as I walked by him to go inside. I wanted to laugh too, but I knew Daddy was not in the mood for anyone to find Uncle Buck amusing. I smiled to myself and kept my head bowed.

Inside the house, my brother and sister gathered around to see the great Uncle Buck. But Daddy wasn't having it. "You kids go on outside and play!" he yelled.

"Oh come on, Curtis, let me see my nieces and nephew," Uncle Buck pleaded.

Daddy shook his head. "If you weren't out doing God knows what you'd have seen them already."

"Curtis, I've been out making money, baby," Uncle Buck said.

Daddy looked at him and rolled his eyes. Daddy never did like the way Uncle Buck made his money. At the time, I had no clue what way that was. All I knew was that Uncle Buck always had on expensive looking clothes and drove the best cars. He managed to get Vivian to New York after her mother died some years back. Vivian wanted to live in the big city and be a star. Uncle Buck said if that's what his baby girl wanted, then that's what she'd get. Mama and Daddy thought Vivian was too young. But Uncle Buck said that his baby was going to be a star and would not spend the rest of her life living in some racist, dead-end town.

Vivian had been gone for about two years now, and from the sound of her letters she had done just want she wanted to do. She said Uncle Buck always sent her money even though he hardly came around to see her. I envied Vivian's life and wanted to do all the things she talked about in her letters. Unfortunately, I was stuck in that racist, dead-end town.

***

After dinner, all the kids gathered in the living room to listen to Uncle Buck's stories about his adventures. Daddy sat at the dining room table looking completely disgusted. The more animated Uncle Buck became, the angrier it made Daddy. He clearly didn't believe a word of what Uncle Buck was saying but my siblings and I ate it up. We lingered on every single word that came out of his mouth. Uncle Buck had the best stories and he knew how to tell them, too. When Daddy finally had enough he jumped up from the dining room table and said, "You kids go on and get ready for bed."

"Awww, Daddy," my sister and brother said in unison.

"'Awww' nothing. Y'all know y'all don't stay up this late," Daddy said.

"Why Mae don't have to go to bed?" Buddy asked, giving me the evil eye. For some reason he thought being ten years old meant that we were the same age. Mama said that was because Daddy treated him like an adult, always giving him grown up tasks to do. He thought if I stayed up late that meant he should be up, too. Normally, Daddy would let him get away with it, but not this time.

"Cause Mae's older," Daddy answered. "But she do got to help y'all get ready for bed," he added.

"Daddy!" I yelled.

"Don't 'Daddy' me. Go on, get," he instructed.

Mama walked out of the kitchen just then and motioned for me to leave. As I left, I turned to look at the three of them gathering in the living room. I knew that Daddy and Uncle Buck were about to argue, and I was not about to miss that for anything in the world.

✳✳✳

I yelled at my brother and sister to hurry up. The sooner they got into bed the sooner I could go back out and listen to Daddy and Uncle Buck go at each other. It seemed like Buddy was intent on working my nerves. He took his sweet time brushing his teeth and putting on his pajamas.

"Come on, Buddy. Hurry up!" I yelled.

"I'm moving as fast as I can," he said, giving me a side-eye.

"No, you're not," I said. "You're moving slow on purpose."

"Am not!" he protested.

"Are so!" I yelled.

Buddy walked past me half dressed in pajamas like I wasn't even talking to him. I wanted to wrap my hands around his neck but thought better. All I needed was for Buddy to cry out and have Daddy come in here and give us all a whipping. I sat on the edge of Franny's bed frowning. It never took Buddy this long to get into bed. Franny must have seen how pissed off I was because she put her little hands on my shoulder and said "Mae, don't mind Buddy. He's just being a brat."

"I know Franny. I know," I replied.

"I ain't being no brat," Buddy said under his breath.

"Yes, you are," I said to him.

Finally, Buddy got tired of hearing my mouth and he put on his pajama shirt and got in his bed. Just as I got up to leave, Franny stopped me and asked in her sweetest little girl voice, "Mae, could you read me a story?"

I could never tell Franny no. That little face shined so bright that it made my heart melt every single time.

"Alright, Franny. But a quick one."

Franny handed me her favorite book and curled up under her blanket. After five minutes of reading both she and Buddy were fast asleep.

By the time I got back in the living room Mama was in the kitchen cleaning, Daddy was laying down on the sofa with his pipe in his mouth, and Uncle Buck was gone.

"Where did Uncle Buck go?" I asked Mama as she came back into the living room, drying her hands on her apron.

"He said something about having some people to see. Who knows with your Uncle," she replied. "Now go on, go to bed. Ain't no sense trying to wait on him."

I reluctantly went to bed wondering if we would see Uncle Buck again. I knew the odds of him sticking around till the morning were slim to none, but I still had hope. By the way Mama was peeking out of the window, I knew she had hope, too.

Better Off Dead

The next morning I woke up early and ran to look out the living room window. A part of me hoped that Uncle Buck's car would be sitting in the driveway, which would mean he was sound asleep in the guest room. But his car wasn't there. All I saw was Daddy and Buddy in their matching overalls heading towards the fields. Disappointment set in as I realized that Uncle Buck was gone and I hadn't even had the chance to tell him goodbye. I even had a letter I wrote for Vivian that I wanted him to take to her. I wanted to tell her all about what I was up to, although I knew it wasn't half as exciting as her life in New York.

"Now, you know how your Uncle do. Ain't no need to stand in front of that window," Mama said from behind me.

"I know, Mama," I sighed. "I just thought I'd take a look. He didn't say goodbye."

"I know, baby. Come on, let's go get some work done before your Daddy gets back," Mama said.

Franny, Mama and I cleaned and cooked for almost an hour. Suddenly, the front door flung open. There stood Uncle Buck. He looked a mess. His nice suit was covered in dirt like he'd slept outside all night. His shirt was hanging out of his pants and his hat was misshapen as if it had been stepped on.

"Good Lord, Buck!" Mama exclaimed. "What you done got yourself into now?"

"Aw, sis, I'm alright," he chuckled. "Ain't nothing a little shower can't take care of."

"Well, get on in the bathroom and wash up before Curtis gets back," Mama told him.

Uncle Buck passed by me and Franny, giving each of us a hug and a kiss. Mama looked at him, shaking her head. But I could tell that she was happy to see him. Everyone, except Daddy, was always happy to see Uncle Buck. I turned to look out the window to see if he and Buddy were on their way back, but they must have still been out in the fields. That was a relief because I knew that

Daddy would lose it if he saw Uncle Buck looking the way he did.

When I heard the shower turn on I ran into Uncle Buck's room. I got his dirty clothes and took them out back to hide them with the rest of the laundry on the porch. Mama always washed the clothes every other day and Daddy stayed clear of anything he viewed as "woman's work." Dirty laundry was one of those things. I figured Daddy would come home and just assume that Uncle Buck spent the night at a friend's house. He didn't have to know how Uncle Buck looked when he walked in the house this morning.

After a while when Uncle Buck hadn't returned to the living room, Mama went to go see what he was doing. She saw he was sound asleep on the bed. He didn't even take the time to cover himself up. Mama took a blanket out of the closet and threw it over him. She looked concerned when she came into the kitchen.

"What's wrong, Mama?" I asked.

"Oh nothing. I guess I'm just thinking about what Buck done gone and got himself into last night," she replied.

"What do you mean?" I asked. Mama and Daddy always talked about how Uncle Buck always got himself into something. But they never said what that something was.

"Buck always wanted good things…a good life. But he never wanted to work hard for it, not like most folk do," she explained. "He just thought things should come to him, like he deserved it more than most. Living that kind of life is dangerous. Don't nothing in life just come to you. You got to go out there, roll up your sleeves, and break your back to get it. Buck never got that. Even when we were kids he took so many chances. My mama used to say she would rather see him dead than to live such a miserable, unsettled life."

Mama looked off into the distance, her eyes were not focused on anything in particular. "I used to get so mad at her for saying that. But now I think I get it."

I looked over at Mama as tears filled her eyes. She loved Uncle Buck, but to say he would be better off dead seemed strange to me. How bad could a person be to actually feel that they would be better off dead?

Paved in Gold

Daddy and Buddy were still in the fields when Uncle Buck finally woke up. I could hear him talking to Mama in the living room while Franny and I were out back doing our chores. I couldn't make out what they were saying, but I figured it couldn't be anything serious since I heard Uncle Buck chuckle every now and then.

Franny got distracted from her chores like always and started running around the yard playing. I stayed on the back porch to watch her. I felt a touch on my shoulder. When I looked up I saw Uncle Buck standing over me, smiling. "What you up to, Lil Bit?" he asked.

"Nothing, just watching Franny," I replied

"Ain't much to do around these parts," Uncle Buck said as he sat down next to me putting a long pipe in his mouth.

"Sho' ain't," I responded.

"That's why I stay on the move," he said. "There's too much world out there to see."

Intrigued, I turned to him and asked, "What's New York like, Uncle Buck?"

"Why you asking about New York?" he asked me.

"I don't know. It just seems like a magical place," I answered.

"New York got its good parts. I mean, a Negro can walk around without being scared that some white devil gonna come up behind him and hang him for just being black. We can just be ourselves. Not like in this hick town." He looked around the yard with disgust. "There's opportunities there for the Negro. The streets are damn near paved in gold and the Negro dresses like they're important like they got important places to go."

"Wow," I said, imagining myself walking down golden streets.

"You know, I'm headed up there to see your cousin, Vivian," he said. "Why don't you come with me? I could use the company."

The thought of going with Uncle Buck to New York made my insides start to dance. But I knew there was no way that Daddy would let me go across the street with Uncle Buck, let alone all the way to New York. "I can't," I said, lowering my head in disappointment.

"Why not? Because of Curtis? Shoot, Lil Bit, you can't let your Daddy's fears be your fears. You got to start living the life you want. Curtis has decided that this is the life he wants, but that don't mean you have to live it with him. That's why I let Vivian go. She had to find where she belonged and so do you, Lil Bit."

"That all sounds good, Uncle Buck, but Daddy ain't never going to let me step foot out of this house."

"How about you and I both talk to him," Uncle Buck suggested. "He may be so busy yelling at me that he might forget about what you asking him." He laughed and gave me a hug.

✳✳✳

I spent the rest of the day thinking about life in New York. I could see myself on stage, singing to real people, not church folk. I would be wearing those fancy clothes that made you look important like you got someplace important to go. I was ready to go. I couldn't wait.

"Good Lord, Mae! You about to burn the chicken!" Mama yelled, interrupting my daydream.

"Sorry, Mama!" I tried to quickly take the chicken out of the darkening oil.

Daddy and Buddy came into the house just as Mama grabbed the frying pan out of my hand to make the chicken herself. Buddy came into the kitchen, all dirty and stinking. "What's burning?" Buddy yelled.

"Your sister burned the chicken," Mama answered. Buddy snickered.

I wanted to pick something up and throw it at him. But Daddy walked in and stood behind Buddy. He'd heard Mama and he, too, had a smile on his face at my expense.

"You ain't gonna keep no husband like that, Mae. Don't no man want no woman who can't cook a decent meal," Daddy said.

I wanted to tell him that I didn't want a husband. I wanted to go to New York and walk on those streets of gold and be one of the important people. But I knew Daddy wouldn't care. Like Uncle Buck said, all Daddy knew was this little town.

I tried to ignore Daddy and Buddy's snickering. Just then Uncle Buck came running in with Franny giggling on his back like he was her own personal horse. He sat Franny down on a chair, looked around and asked, "What y'all in here laughing about?"

"Mae burning the chicken. Daddy said she ain't gonna keep no husband not knowing how to cook," Buddy explained.

"Oh hell, Lil Bit, don't you pay that no mind," Uncle Buck said. "You gonna be one of them modern women who don't need no man,"

"Oh Buck, you talking crazy," Mama said.

"No, I'm not, sis," Uncle Buck replied.

"You always talk crazy, Buck," Daddy said as he turned to walk out the kitchen.

"You know what your problem is, Curtis?" Uncle Buck asked, following Daddy. "You think everyone in the world lives like you in this small, hick town. You know, there are women out there that don't spend their life in no kitchen. Hell, they work just like men do."

"That ain't no woman I know. Men work and women take care of the home. That's how it goes. Don't come up in my house filling my kid's heads with all kinds of nonsense," Daddy said.

By this time we were all standing in the living room, watching as Daddy and Uncle Buck talked about what kind of woman I should be.

"It ain't nonsense, Curtis. There are women out there living the life. If you'd get a TV in this old shack you'd see that," Uncle Buck said.

"Well, the women in this shack live a pretty damn good life, Buck," Daddy shot back. "Don't nobody in this shack want nothing to do with your world and the fast women who live in it."

"That ain't true, Curtis," Uncle Buck said. "It seems to me that Mae wants more than this little shack. And I think she should come with me tomorrow morning when I leave."

Daddy stood up and looked as if he was ten feet tall. He towered over Uncle Buck, overwhelmed with rage.

Mama must have felt it because she ran to stand between the two of them.

"Now, I know you're not standing in my home telling me you taking *my* daughter with you?" Daddy asked. His eyes were wide, voice booming.

"Curtis, calm down," Mama said, holding on to his arm.

"Curtis, there's a world out there for Mae. She can do anything she wants. She can go to school, she can start a career. Hell, she can even sing and be a big star," Uncle Buck said, standing toe-to-toe with Daddy.

Daddy reached out and grabbed Uncle Buck's collar. Mama flinched and yelled, "Curtis!"

Uncle Buck's expression changed to one of panic. He'd always laughed Daddy off, but this time, he wasn't laughing. I guess he knew Daddy wasn't playing.

"You gonna get the hell out my house, Buck, but Mae ain't going with you! You hear me?" Daddy yelled as Mama tried to pry his hands from around Uncle Buck's collar.

"Come on, Curtis," Uncle Buck pleaded. "That should be Mae's choice." He tried to break free of Daddy's grasp.

"Mae! Tell this scoundrel you ain't going nowhere with him," Daddy demanded, still holding on to Uncle Buck.

I didn't speak. Tears streamed down my face. The words were caught in my throat and all that would come out was a whimper. Franny wrapped her little arms around my waist and Mama looked at me, waiting for a response.

"Mae!" Daddy yelled again.

"Mae, you answer your daddy," Mama said.

I lowered my head and wiped the tears from my cheeks. I said softly, "I want to go."

Ain't No Turning Back

I barely slept. I spent most of the night packing so I'd be ready to leave with Uncle Buck. I woke up before sunrise and ran into the living room, hoping to catch Daddy before he and Buddy went into the fields. But the first person to come out their bedroom was Mama. She stared at me with sad eyes and a half smile. I knew she didn't want me to go either. I knew she and Daddy were disappointed in my choice. In that moment, I was disappointed in my choice, too. I curled up on the sofa and buried my head in the cushions.

"Mae," Mama said quietly. "I think your uncle will be ready to leave soon. You should go get your things." Her voice was emotionless.

"Yes ma'am," I replied. The sadness on Mama's face consumed me and I began to sob as I walked to my room. The tears fell fast and hard. It finally hit me that I was about to leave the only place I'd ever lived. North Carolina was my home. All my family and memories were here. It was all I knew. I wanted to tell everyone that I changed my mind. But Uncle Buck came into my room before I could do so.

"Hey, Lil Bit! You ready?"

"Uncle Buck, I ...," I began.

"Don't do that, Lil Bit," Uncle Buck said, wiping away my tears. "This is a good thing. You'll see."

"But everyone's mad at me," I cried.

"This ain't their life, Lil Bit. It's yours," he said. "If something deep in you is telling you to go, then you need to listen to that. Don't worry about anybody else."

I smiled at him, grabbed my bag, and followed him out of my bedroom. By the time we got outside Mama and Franny were already standing on the porch waiting for us. Uncle Buck grabbed my bag and took it to his car. Franny ran to me and wrapped her arms around me so tight that she nearly made me lose my balance.

"I'ma miss you, Mae," she said, tears streaming down her face.

I lifted her up in my arms and held her tightly as she rested her head on my shoulder.

"I'll miss you, too. I love you, Franny."

"I love you, too," Franny said, giving me a kiss on the cheek. I put Franny down and slowly walked over to Mama. She handed me a brown paper bag.

"Here are some sandwiches I made for the two of you. It's a long ride. You may get hungry."

As I reached for the bag she pulled me into her arms. I could feel Mama's tears as they landed on my neck. She whispered in my ear, "You be careful, baby."

"I will, Mama. I promise." I broke away from her warm embrace and wiped away my tears.

Mama looked at me as if she was trying to memorize every inch of my face. She ran her fingers through my hair, then down my cheeks.

"I'll be back, Mama," I said, clutching her hands.

The front door flung open and Daddy walked out of the house with Buddy following close behind, dressed in their matching overalls. Daddy stood next to me, but he didn't look at me.

"I'll be out in the fields," he said to Mama.

He went down the porch steps and into the yard. I don't know what came over me in that moment. I wanted Daddy to look at me, to tell me he'd miss me. I shouted, "Bye, Daddy! I'll miss you!"

He stopped walking for a second but didn't turn around. He yelled, "Let's go, Buddy!" Buddy jumped off the porch and ran to Daddy. I did the same, grabbing his arm.

"Daddy, please! I'm sorry."

Daddy looked down at my hand on his arm. Then he looked away again. "Ain't no looking back." He pulled my hand away and walked towards the fields.

Buddy started to follow but stopped mid-way and ran back. He threw his arms around me. "Bye, Mae. I'll miss you." Then he ran to catch up with Daddy.

I stood there feeling empty and rejected, second guessing my decision. The thought of Daddy not being able to look me in the eye destroyed every inch of my being. Uncle Buck put his arm around my shoulders. "Come on, Lil Bit. Let's go."

I followed him to the car and got in. I looked through the window at Mama and Franny standing on the porch with tears in their eyes. I waved at them. Franny waved back and Mama blew me a kiss. She yelled to her brother, "Take care of my baby, Buck."

"With my life, sis. I promise." He blew her and Franny a kiss, got in the car and drove off.

I must have cried myself to sleep because by the time I woke up we were driving on a lonely road I didn't recognize. Uncle Buck had the music turned up loud, bopping his head to the beat. When he saw that I was awake he turned the radio down.

"Well, good morning, Lil Bit. You feel refreshed?" he let out a chuckle, bringing a smile to my face. Uncle Buck's laugh always made me smile. It was loud and joyful like he didn't have a care in the world. He'd always let it out so effortlessly, calming everyone around him. I loved that about Uncle Buck. He made everything seem like it was going to be alright.

"I guess so," I replied.

"Good, because you gonna need to be. There's a whole world waiting for you out there, Lil Bit. You gonna have to be ready to reach out and grab it!"

"Ain't nothing out there, Uncle Buck. Just a change of scenery." I leaned my head against the window.

"Oh, now don't you get like your Daddy on me. You know better than that. You know why I call you Lil Bit?"

I shook my head. "Not really."

"Because when you were a little girl you were always asking for a little bit of something," Uncle Buck said, chuckling again. "I don't care what anybody had, you would always ask 'Can I have a Lil Bit?' Boy, I tell you. I always knew you were going to get out of that place. You were going to be the one to show this family that there's a little bit of something more out there in the world."

"What if I don't find it?" I asked. "What if all this was for nothing?"

"God don't lead you somewhere for nothing. Now, don't tell your mama I said that. She may think I done gone and got saved or something," he said, laughing at himself.

"I guess so," I reluctantly agreed.

"You're gonna be alright, Lil Bit. You'll see." He squeezed my hand for reassurance. "You're gonna be alright."

The sun was shining bright and the warm breeze blew gently through the open window. It made me feel like everything Uncle Buck said made sense, as if God was smiling down and giving me His permission. I felt like something new and exciting was coming. Maybe Uncle Buck was right. My heart was telling me there was something wonderful on the way. I couldn't wait to get to New York and find out what it was. I just knew God had something special planned for me.

Some time later, Uncle Buck said he had to make a stop in Virginia. He pulled off the main highway onto a dirt road that seemed to lead to nowhere. I looked around, trying to figure out where we were but I had no clue.

"Where are we going?" I asked him.

"I just got a little business I got to take care of. Ain't nothing for you to worry about," he said.

We rode down that dirt road for a while before we finally came to what looked to be a little town. It had small buildings and even smaller roads. Uncle Buck turned down another road hidden by trees. At the clearing, there was a tiny house. A group of black men sat on the porch, talking and smoking cigarettes. The men seemed to range from all ages with the littlest one soaking in every bit of his surroundings.

Uncle Buck parked right in front of the porch and told me to stay in the car. He got out and walked over to the men. They all seemed to know Uncle Buck judging by the way they took turns shaking his hand and giving him hugs when he walked up to them. They talked for a moment with serious expressions on their faces. I wondered why they were all suddenly serious. Uncle Buck turned to look at me, giving me a wink before walking off with a younger man who looked to be close to my age.

I followed Uncle Buck and the young man with my eyes until I lost them when they walked behind the house and into the woods. I turned back towards the men still left on the porch. They looked concerned. One of them took the little one inside the house and closed the door. Another gave me a smile and a nod.

I got a terrible feeling in the pit of my stomach. Something was wrong. I looked around. I needed to leave but had no clue where to go. The men began pacing back and forth, looking towards the woods. The more they paced the more nervous I became.

Like a bolt of lightning Uncle Buck and the young man came running out of the woods from behind the house. The other men all ran into the house, closing the door behind them. Uncle Buck flung open my car door and yelled for me to get out. He went to the back, popped the trunk and opened my bag. He pulled two brown packets from his pocket and stuck them in my bag before handing it to me.

"Now, Lil Bit, these here are for you and Vivian. Don't you open it until you get to her. You hear me?" Uncle Buck asked, trying to catch his breath.

"What's going on? Aren't you coming?" I was terrified.

"I don't think so, Lil Bit. That's my friend over there." Uncle Buck nodded at the young man. He stood about five feet away and stared at the woods. "He's gonna make sure you get there."

"But why?" I was confused. "Why can't you take me?"

"Lil Bit, sometimes life catches up to you. I guess it's my turn now," he said.

"We got to go!" said the young man as he ran up to us.

Uncle Buck kissed me on the forehead. "Go where God takes you, Lil Bit." Then he slammed the trunk lid, hopped in his car and sped off. The young man snatched my bag, grabbed my hand and took off running, dragging me behind him. We hid behind an old barn next to an even older pick-up truck.

I heard noises that sounded like speeding cars and gunfire. A man yelled, "Get that nigger!"

It was quiet again. The young man slowly looked around the side of the barn. He grabbed my hand again. "All clear. Let's go."

He led me to the old pick-up truck and opened the passenger door for me to get in.

"Where's Uncle Buck? What's going on?" I asked him.

"I promise I'll explain later. Right now we got to get out of here," he said softly. His big hazel eyes looked deep into mine, reassuring me that it was safe to go with him and that he'd take care of me. I got in the truck and he closed the door behind me. I watched as he pulled a cap from his back pocket and placed it on his head. He took off his brown, long sleeved work shirt, threw it in the back of the truck, leaving him in a white t-shirt.

He slowly drove down a dirt road, different than the one Uncle Buck brought us on, until we reached the main road. My eyes caught sight of what looked to be a small fire. I leaned in closer against the window and realized that it was Uncle Buck's car. I searched everywhere but didn't see Uncle Buck. Frightened, I began to cry. Then, a group of white men, laughing, came out of the woods dragging something behind them.

It took me no time at all to realize they were dragging Uncle Buck. He was battered and bleeding.

"Stop the car!" I yelled. "We got to help him!"

"Are you crazy!" the young man yelled back, pulling me away from the window. "They'll kill us!"

I jerked away from him and looked out of the window again. I was determined to help my uncle even if it meant jumping out of a moving truck. As the truck got closer, Uncle Buck lifted his head. Blood dripped from his face. He looked directly at me, gave me a wink and mouthed, "I love you."

At that moment a fat, sweaty, white man lifted a shotgun to Uncle Buck's head and pulled the trigger. The sound of the gun echoed through the air, smoke curling up towards the sky. Uncle Buck's limp body fell to the dusty ground. I covered my mouth with trembling hands to keep from screaming. The young man sped up the truck, trying to hurry past the scene, but the sight of Uncle Buck being murdered was forever stuck in my mind. Uncle Buck was dead.

Hi, I'm Charles

For hours I sat in silence in that old pick-up truck as we drove down an empty highway. My face was stained with tears, my eyes swollen shut from crying. Every time the truck backfired I almost jumped out of my skin. The young man with me would say, "It's alright, it's just the truck."

But it wasn't alright. Nothing was ever going to be alright. How was I going to tell Mama that her only brother was gone? How was I going to tell Vivian?

I closed my eyes and laid my head against the window, praying to get rid of the image of Uncle Buck lying bloody and motionless on the side of the road. I could still see those white men laughing and patting each other on the back, as if killing my uncle was a momentous victory, as if he didn't matter. I wondered if that was the world that Uncle Buck was so desperate for me to see. The world where my life meant nothing, where my body lying dead in the dirt was cause for joy. If that was the world then I wanted no parts of it. I was content with singing in a little church on a dusty road and living in a little house far away from everyone. The tears started to fall again.

The young man pulled the truck off the road and parked in front of a busy diner. There were other young people like me, going in and out, talking and laughing. I couldn't really focus on any of them and I didn't care. All I wanted was to be somewhere I felt safe. Whether that meant going to Vivian's or turning back around and going home, it didn't matter at that point. I wanted the terrible images out of my head. But most of all, I wanted Uncle Buck back.

"Where are we?" I asked as he opened the passenger door for me to get out.

"This is D.C., the capital city," he said with a smile.

"What are we doing here? Why aren't we in New York?"

"We got a few more hours left before we get to New York. I figured you might want to stop to use the restroom and get a bite to eat," he said, pointing at the diner.

I hadn't realized how hungry I was until he mentioned it. It dawned on me that the food Mama had packed for me and Uncle Buck was left in his car when they burned it. I hadn't eaten any of it.

✳✳✳

When I came out of the restroom I saw the young man already sitting and talking to a waitress. I also saw a payphone hanging on the wall in front of me. I grabbed it and called my parents collect. I heard Daddy say "Hello" just before the operator said, "You have a collect call from…"

"Daddy, please help!" I cried, right before the operator asked if he would accept the charges. He said no and hung up the phone.

I stood there shaking, still holding the phone receiver in my hand. I was so mad at Uncle Buck for leaving me like this. I was stuck with some man I didn't know going only God knows where. How did I even know he was going to take me to New York? There was a voice in my head telling me that I may never get to Vivian and it would all be my fault. I should've stayed home and not followed Uncle Buck. Now here I was, all alone.

I composed myself, put the receiver back on the hook, and walked over to the table where the young man was sitting. I sat across from him and folded my arms. I wanted him to know I was not to be messed with.

"Are you doing alright now?" he asked as he tried to make eye contact with me.

"I don't know." I turned my head from his direction to look through the window at the street.

"I know that was probably a silly question. I mean what happened backed there was...I don't know. Your uncle was a good man," he said.

"The best," I replied, wiping away tears from my eyes.

"Hey, don't do that." He handed me a napkin. "I promise you, everything's gonna be alright."

"You can't make that type of promise," I said.

"Sure I can. I mean shoot, if you can't trust a country boy from the bayou of Louisiana, then who can you trust?" he asked, smiling.

My lack of response must have been loud enough to deflate his attempt at humor because he was suddenly serious. He stretched his hand across the table to shake mine. "How about we start with an introduction. Hi, I'm Charles. Charles Dupuy."

I turned away from the window to look at him and slowly stretched out my hand to meet his. "I'm Mae."

"Nice to officially meet you, Miss Mae," he said shaking my hand.

His grip was firm but gentle. The roughness of his palm made it clear that he worked with his hands, but the rest of his light skin looked smooth. I lifted my gaze to meet his perfect, hazel eyes as they smiled at me. I almost got lost in those eyes. His short, wavy hair complimented the well-defined structure of his masculine face. I'd never seen a man so beautiful. Never knew Negros looked this way. I almost lost my breath looking at him. The feeling was so overwhelming that I had to quickly pull my hand away and break eye contact.

"Nice to meet you, too," I said, trying my best not to look at him.

Just then the waitress came with our food. I looked at the plate sitting in front of me wondering how she knew what to bring since I hadn't ordered anything. Charles must have read the expression on my face because he quickly explained, "I had her bring us both some fries and a burger. Hope that's alright with you, Miss Mae."

"It's alright," I answered, popping a fry into my mouth.

Charles busied himself dressing his burger with a whole bunch of ketchup and mustard. He looked so excited to eat the food that it made me chuckle a bit to myself. I looked around the diner, noticing for the first time how different this place looked from anything I'd seen before. The young people were so poised and put together. They walked around confidently, with their books in their hands, looking like young intellectuals.

"What is this place? I asked Charles.

"Oh, this here is the great Howard University," he said as I looked at the people surrounding us.

"What makes it so great?" I asked.

"Because it's where all the best black minds come from. Or so they tell me. I ain't nowhere close to being a great black mind," he said with a grin.

"I ain't never heard of it," I said, looking at the big brick buildings looming across the street.

"Yeah, well, Howard is where all educated blacks want to be," he said before taking a bite of his burger.

"This where you want to come?" I asked.

"Oh no, not me, Miss Mae," he said, shaking his head. "I barely finished eighth grade. I'm a man who works with my hands. Books ain't for me."

"Well, it's a beautiful place," I said, still admiring the buildings across the street.

"Yeah, it is," Charles agreed. "You know, I always say if I was to ever have kids I'd make sure they go here. Ain't no sense in them ending up like me."

I looked at him again. "What do you mean 'ending up like you'?"

"Well," he said, taking a long pause and putting down his burger. "I mean I drift…you know…just looking for work. It ain't no easy life. That's why I'm headed to New York. I hear there's plenty of work there. They say a man could finally settle down and make a good living."

"Who are you going to see? I mean where will you live?" I asked.

"Oh, don't worry about me, Miss Mae. I got a friend up there name Fred. I'ma stay with him at least until I get on my feet. Besides, thanks to your uncle, I already got a couple of dollars in my pocket to get me started."

"What?" How did he do that?" I didn't understand.

"I met him when I got into North Carolina and he sent me ahead to Virginia. He said he had some friends out there who would be happy to give me some work. Sho' enough, when I got there they put me to work. Now it probably wasn't the most legal work, but all I wanted was some money to get me to New York," he explained.

I asked, "Is the illegal work what got my uncle killed?"

"You could say that," Charles confirmed. "Your uncle owed those white men some money and they weren't about to let no Negro go without paying."

I was angry. "Uncle Buck died because of some stupid money?!"

"Yeah. I think he saw it coming because he wrote down an address on a piece of paper and made me promise to get you there," he said.

"Why didn't he just give them the money?" I asked.

"I don't know," Charles said. "It was a lot of money. Maybe he didn't have it."

"He didn't have to stop there. We could have just kept on going," I replied.

Charles nodded. "Yeah, you could've. Not sure why he did. I reckon he knew those white men would always be looking for him. Maybe they knew where his family was, maybe he came back for me. Not sure, Miss Mae. But like I said, your uncle was a good man.

I sat there, eating slowly and thinking about what Charles said about Uncle Buck. It was clear that he admired him, but I was still so angry. All he had to do was keep on driving. He didn't have to stop. He didn't have to do anything but get us to New York. If he had, we would be there by now and he would be alive.

When we finished eating Charles paid the check. We got back in the pickup truck and took off for New York.

He was a Good Man

I felt Charles' hand tugging gently on my shoulder, pulling me out of my sleep. "Miss Mae. We're here."

I rubbed my eyes, sat up straight and looked around. I was instantly overwhelmed by the sound of the cars rushing by and all the people crowding the sidewalks. I couldn't keep up with all that was happening, my head swiveling back and forth in a panic as I tried to take it all in.

"You alright, Miss Mae?" Charles asked.

"I don't know where I'm supposed to go," I said nervously.

"Come on, I'll take you." Charles got out of the truck and headed to the back to get my bag.

I stood outside of the passenger door, afraid to move. People passed me by, looking at me as if I didn't belong. My old, dull, brown plaid dress was no match for their fancy, light-colored clothes. Charles came over and took my hand. He led me through a crowd of people as we made our way to a door hidden between two stores. Charles rang the buzzer and we waited until a voice on the other end said, "Yea. Who is it?" I immediately recognized the voice. It was Vivian.

"It's me Viv!" I yelled back into the box that hung on the wall next to the door.

"Oh my God! Mae, is that you?!" Vivian yelled back. "I'm coming. I'm coming. Wait! I'm coming!"

Vivian's voice put a smile on my face. Finally, something was going right. I looked at Charles. He smiled back at me.

"I reckon I held up my promise, Miss Mae," Charles said.

"Yes, you did. Thank you," I said. "Will I see you again?"

"I don't see why not." He grinned and handed over my bag.

The door opened almost knocking me over. Charles grabbed me and pulled me out of the way. Vivian appeared, screaming and jumping. She flung her arms around me and squeezed me tight.

"Oh God, Mae! I can't believe you're here!" she said.

"I can't believe it myself," I said, looking back at Charles.

"Oh my Lord. Wait, where's Daddy?" she asked, looking past me and Charles.

"Um…" I didn't know what to say.

"Well, ladies I have to go. Y'all should get on inside anyway," Charles interrupted. I guess he figured if I had to break the news to Vivian that her dad was dead, doing so in the middle of the street was not the best way.

"Oh, and who might you be?" Vivian asked as she gazed seductively at Charles.

"This is Charles, Vivian," I said.

"Well, hello there, Charles." Vivian gave him her best smile.

"Nice to meet you, Miss Vivian," Charles said, shaking her hand. Then he turned to me and tipped the brim of his cap. "Take care, Miss Mae."

As Charles walked away I wondered if I would ever see him again. I wondered what he would do and where he would go. Oddly, I already missed him.

"That sho' is a fine man!" Vivian said, leading me through the door and looking over my shoulder at Charles.

We walked up a long flight of stairs before reaching her small apartment. Vivian took my bag and plopped it on one of the two small beds in the room. Then she looked around and said "Well, here it is. It ain't much but it does the job. This will be your bed and we can share the closet and the dresser. The bathroom is down the hall."

"I like it," I said, shrugging my shoulders and giving her a smile.

"Good. Man, look at you Mae. You're all grown up now!" She pulled me into another hug.

I almost burst into tears as she held me. But I knew I had to hold myself together. I needed to tell Vivian what happened to Uncle Buck and crying like a crazy person was not gonna help anybody.

She let go of me and went over to the window, pulling the curtains aside and looking outside. "So, where is Daddy? Is he up to his tricks again? He probably left you and drove off. That man ain't never been 'bout nothing," Vivian said as she peered down at the streets below.

I walked over to her, took her by the hand and led her to one of the beds. We sat down next to each other. I looked Vivian in the eyes and told her everything. When I was done I waited for her to say something. To get sad or mad or maybe even to scream. But her face was blank. She sat motionless and looked straight ahead at the bare white walls.

"Viv, are you alright?" I asked as tears started to run down my face.

"I…yeah…I think so. I just always knew this day would come. But now that it's here I'm not sure how to feel," she said.

I put my arm around her shoulders and held her tight. I didn't know what to say to help her make sense of it all.

"Oh, Mae," Vivian said, rubbing my back, "that must have been just awful for you."

I sobbed. "I wanted to get out of that truck and help. I swear I did, Viv."

"Oh, come on now, Mae. What would you have done among all those white men? Y'all did the right thing to keep on driving. Daddy wouldn't have wanted you to stop," Vivian said.

I pulled away from her wiping the tears from my eyes. "Maybe but…I don't know."

"You were right to keep on moving," she assured me, holding me in her arms.

We held on to each other for what seemed like an eternity. Then Vivian broke free and said, "Let's get you unpacked and settled."

I opened my bag and we unpacked my clothes. The two brown packets fell out. "What are these?" Vivian asked as she picked them up.

"Oh, Uncle Buck said that one was for me and the other was for you. He didn't say what was in them," I told her.

"Well, let's see." She handed one to me.

Inside each packet were fresh one hundred dollar bills. Vivian's jaw dropped and her eyes grew wide at the sight.

"Oh my God, Viv! How much is it?" I asked.

Vivian quickly counted the money and when she was done her eyes grew wider.

"There's ten thousand dollars here," she said.

"What!?" I was shocked.

Vivian grabbed the other packet out of my hand so she could count the money inside. When she was done she handed it back to me. "You have ten thousand, too."

We stared at each other. We were stunned. We didn't know what to do or say until finally, Vivian broke the silence with a roar of laughter. She jumped around the room.

Then it dawned on me. "Viv! Vivian!" I yelled, trying to get her attention.

"What?" she yelled back.

"This is it," I said in a panic.

"This is what?" she asked.

"Charles said that Uncle Buck owed those white men some money. That he died because he didn't pay up," I explained.

"So?" she asked, plopping back down beside me on the bed.

"So, this is the money he owed them," I said. "This is why he was killed!"

"Wait. You're saying that my daddy owed these white men twenty grand and rather than pay them back so they wouldn't kill him, he gave it to us?" Vivian asked.

"Yeah," I said smiling to myself. "That is exactly what I'm saying."

"My daddy wouldn't…would he?" she said, looking down at the money.

I nodded. "He did, Viv. He did."

"Oh my lord." She grabbed her money, laid back on the bed and squeezed it against her chest as if she was hugging someone.

I walked over to the window and looked out at the city. Charles' words echoed through my head. My Uncle Buck, he was a good man.

Go Where God Leads Me

A couple of days went by and I hadn't figured out what to do with my life in New York. Vivian was working all hours of the night at some dive bar a couple of blocks over. She invited me down there a few times but I didn't think I was ready for that part of New York life. Every once in a while, during the day while Vivian slept, I ventured outside to see what was going on.

The old white man at the store downstairs below Vivian's apartment had taken a liking to me and asked if I would like to work there a couple of days a week. He said he knew what it was like to be a stranger in a new place since he and his wife had just come to New York from Italy. They had a big family but no kids. His wife was often in the store, too, and she would sit and talk to me. She told me all about her life and family in Italy. I loved spending my days with them. The Polamos became like family. They were the nicest people I'd met since coming to New York. They made my time in this strange city a lot more bearable.

It was Mrs. Polamo who convinced me to try calling home again.

"Bella, so much time go by now. Call your familia. They must be sick with worry for you," she said in her thick Italian accent.

When I left their shop that afternoon I stopped by the payphone that was down the hall from Vivian's apartment. This time I decided against calling collect. I picked up the receiver, put my money in and dialed. I prayed that Daddy didn't answer because I knew he would hang up.

"Hello?" said the voice on the other end. It was Mama.

"Mama!" I yelled.

"Oh my God!" Mama cried. "Mae, it's you! Thank you, Jesus!"

"Mama, are you alright," I asked.

"Mae, where have you been? Where are you now?" She was crying at this point.

"I'm with Vivian in New York," I told her.

"What? But how?" she asked. "Some men came by that night when you left and they brought Buck's body. They just dropped it off on the porch like it was nothing. I kept asking them what happened to you but they wouldn't answer. Then your daddy said that you had tried to call earlier asking for help. Oh, baby, I thought you were dead, too!"

"No, Mama. Uncle Buck fixed it so I would be safe and he had someone bring me to New York," I told her.

"Did you know he was dead?" she asked.

"I saw them kill him, Mama." I broke down in tears.

"Oh, baby! Listen. I'm gonna have your daddy send you some money and you gonna take the bus and come back home, ok?" Mama said.

"I can't, Mama."

"Why not, Mae?" the tone of her voice switching from concern to anger.

"Daddy said 'ain't no going back,'" I told her.

"Don't you worry about your daddy. I don't care what your daddy has to say any more," she proclaimed.

"Mama, I got to do this. Please say you understand," I begged.

"I don't, Mae," she replied. "I just want to know that you're home and safe."

"I'm safe, Mama," I assured her. "I just need to go where God leads me."

"And God led you to New York?" she asked.

"I think so, Mama," I said. "I feel like this is where I need to be."

"Ok, Mae. I don't know what else to say. I have to trust you know what you're doing. Just call every day so I know you're alright," she said.

"I promise, Mama, I will. Tell everyone I said hi. I know Daddy don't want to hear from me but could you tell him I love him?" I asked.

"I will, baby. And tell Vivian that we buried her daddy a couple of days ago. We didn't do anything big. Just a quick service with a few family members."

"Yes ma'am, I'll let her know," I promised. "Love you, Mama."

"Love you, too, baby."

I walked back into the apartment with a lighter heart after hanging up the phone. Thanks to Mrs. Polamo, I had made things right with my family. Well, at least with Mama. But knowing that I could call her meant the world to me. I didn't feel so alone anymore.

When I entered the apartment Vivian was still curled up in her bed, fast asleep. I opened the window to let some light in the room. She turned and then sat up in her bed.

"Hey, what's the big idea?" she asked.

"Come on, Viv," I said. "You've been asleep for most of the day."

"Because I worked all night," she said, laying back down.

"Speaking of work, the Polamos asked me to work for them in the store a few days a week. I think I might do it," I told her.

"What for?" she asked.

"Because it's something to do and I need the money," I said.

"No, you don't" she said, jumping out of the bed with a sudden burst of energy. "Did you forget? We're rich!"

"I don't want to spend that money, Viv. I don't feel right about it," I said

"Are you crazy?" she asked. "Hell, I've already been spending mine."

"On what?" I asked.

"The best thing in the world for the both of us," she said, grabbing me and pulling me down onto the bed. "I'm buying a club. Can you imagine me owning the best club New York City has ever seen and you being our featured singer?"

I gasped. "What?! Viv, that's crazy talk!"

"No, it's not. It's our future. This is why Daddy left us the money in the first place," she said. "Not so we can work in some dive bar at night or grocery store during the day. It's so we can live. Don't you want to make all your dreams come true?"

"Yeah, but not with that money," I said.

"Well, I'm going to use it and my club will be bigger and better than the Cotton Club. You'll see." Vivian laid back down on the bed, covering herself up with the blanket.

I shook my head and went over to my bed to lay down. I didn't want to use that money even if it meant me getting to sing. The money seemed tainted. It came from bad blood and I didn't want it on my hands. I know Uncle Buck thought he was doing a good thing, but that money wouldn't bring any good to me or Vivian.

Then I remembered what Mama asked me to do. "Hey, Viv?"

"Yeah?"

"My Mama said they already buried your daddy," I told her. "I'm sorry you missed it."

"Not me," she said. "The only good thing he ever done for me was this money. Guess we even now."

Mrs. Dupuy?

I had been in New York for a few months and, so far, everything was going well. I started working regularly at the Polamos' store and Vivian had finally opened her club. I'd go down there every once in a while but the crowd was a bit much for my taste. The boys were all over the girls, and the girls seemed to like it.

I told Vivian she needed to be careful of who she let into her club, but she said money was money and if they paying she didn't care who came in. I, for one, had no intentions of spending my night in a club where everyone was wild and out of control. It seemed like there was a fight breaking out every five seconds. I worried about Vivian, but she was so excited to have her own club that she didn't care what happened.

The inside of the club was actually really nice. She named it *Buck's*, after her daddy, although I had to convince her to do that. She originally wanted to name it after herself. I told her that if it hadn't been for Uncle Buck, she wouldn't have the club. She finally agreed and *Buck's* was born. There was a big dance floor with a stage at the front surrounded by tables draped with pretty lace cloths.

Buck's had character and people talked about it. Everyone had to come to *Buck's* at least once when they came to New York. While I did worry about what kind of folks came to the club, I was still proud of Vivian for doing what she said she was going to do. I hadn't done that. I came to New York to be a singer and I ended up working in a small grocery store. I'd started to think that New York may have been too much for me. Maybe I wasn't ready for it. Maybe I was just a little country girl with big city dreams, but no big city drive.

I sat around that apartment all alone thinking about what I should do next. Every time I called Mama and she told me about what everyone was up to, I'd get a little home sick. It was hard being away from them, especially since I really wasn't doing much with my time.

I turned on the radio and Ella Fitzgerald's voice came through. I closed my eyes and started to sing out loud with her.

"...there's a someone I'm longing to see.

I hope that he turns out to be someone to watch over me."

There was loud clapping. I ran to turn off the radio.

"Oh my Lord, Mae! Hell, I thought Ella herself was sitting in our apartment," Vivian said as she closed the door behind her.

"God, Vivian, you scared me," I said, feeling a little embarrassed.

"Well, I'm sorry, Mae," Vivian said, "but I had to hear you sing. I'd forgotten how good you were."

"I'm alright."

"No, Mae, you're fantastic. I sho' wish you'd reconsider coming down to my club and singing," she said.

I shook my head. "Vivian, that ain't my kind of scene."

"What do you think your scene is gonna be once you start singing? This is it, honey. You need to go on down to my club and let them hear what you got," she insisted.

"I...no, I can't," I said.

"Well, alright. But can you at least come work for me tonight?" she asked. "My coat-check girl can't make it. I really need you, Mae."

"Ok, but just for tonight," I agreed.

Later that evening Vivian gave me one of her fancy dresses. It was tight and yellow and fell just below my knees. She fixed my hair in an up-do and placed a flower in it.

"This is how coat-check girls dress?" I asked.

"They do in my establishment," she replied.

When we got to the club it was still early and people hadn't arrived yet. Vivian showed me where I would be working and she busied herself with other things. I sat in the coat room and watched as people slowly trickled in, all of them in their fancy clothes with even fancier coats. Pretty soon the place was packed. After a while, Vivian ran into the coat room and said, "Mae, I need you again."

"What happened now?" I asked,

"My singer ain't show up," Vivian said.

"Oh no, Viv!" I said, shaking my head. "You know I said I ain't singing."

"I know what you said, Mae, but I need you. Please, Mae!" The look on Vivian's face made me feel like I had no other option but to help.

"Ok fine, but I don't know what I'm gonna sing," I said reluctantly.

"Sing what you were singing earlier today. Sing Ella," she said with a big smile.

"Ok, I guess."

"Oh thank you Mae!" Vivian jumped up and down. "What are we gonna call you?"

"What do you mean?" I asked. "My name."

"No. Every singer has an exotic name," she said. "You know, something that just rolls off the tongue. You need one of those."

I thought for a minute, but I still liked Mae. I thought it was a nice name but figured maybe adding a last name could help some. The only name that came to mind was one that I liked the moment I heard it. I even liked the person it belonged to.

"How about Mae Dupuy?" I said.

Vivian's face lit up with excitement. "Mae Dupuy. Yes that's it. Mae Dupuy!"

Vivian pulled me by the hand and hurried me backstage. I peeked around the curtains and saw her talking to the band. The band members looked a bit aggravated, but what could they do? Vivian was the boss. I looked away and tried to compose myself, but my nerves were kicking in. My palms were sweating, my stomach was doing flip-flops, and every inch of my body was shaking. I was just about to walk away when I heard Vivian get on the microphone.

"Hi, ladies and gentlemen. Thanks for making it out to *Buck's* tonight. We have a very special treat for you. Making her singing debut tonight is Miss Mae Dupuy!"

The audience clapped and the lights dimmed. I slowly walked from behind the curtains and onto the stage towards Vivian and the microphone. A bright light from above welcomed me with its blinding beam. Vivian whispered in my ear, "You can do this, Mae."

I took a deep breath and heard the band begin to play Ella's song. I opened my mouth and started to sing.

The room was quiet. All eyes were on me. I was so nervous I thought for sure that I would forget the words. But then I looked out into the crowd and saw those perfect hazel eyes looking back at me. I looked deep into them and sang every word of Ella's song just for those eyes.

When it was over the audience roared with applause. Some even whistled. I smiled at the sight of everyone. They enjoyed what I did, they enjoyed me! I floated down the stairs off the stage. Vivian met me at the bottom and gave me a big hug. We walked toward the back of the club.

"You were fantastic, Mae!' Vivian said.

"You really were," said a male voice from behind.

Vivian and I both looked in his direction. "Charles," I said.

"Well, if it isn't my daddy's fine friend," Vivian said.

"Vivian, could you please give us a moment," I asked.

"Sure," she said as she started to walk away. Then she stopped in front of Charles and said, "When you're done, why don't you bring your fine self over to the bar and let me buy you a drink."

"Thanks for the offer, Miss Vivian, but I'm not much of a drinking man," Charles said.

"Well, you sure ain't for me then." Vivian sashayed away.

Charles moved closer to me and I got a better look at those perfect hazel eyes. The eyes I sang to. The eyes that had watched over me from Virginia to New York. The eyes I thought I may never see again. And here they were, right in front of me.

"So what should I call you, Miss Mae? Or are you going by Mrs. Dupuy these days?" Charles said, acknowledging the fact that I used his last name.

I felt so embarrassed. I didn't think I'd see him again and the name was just so perfect for me to use. I never imagined he'd know about it.

"I'm sorry…I just need-."

"It's alright, Miss Mae," he interrupted. "The name fits you beautifully," he said with a smile.

"What have you been up to?" I asked, trying to break the tension.

"That friend of mine I told you about found me a job with the railroads," he explained. "It's pretty good money."

"That's great," I said. "But what are you doing here?"

"Well, I heard about this place called *Buck's* and figured...well, I was hoping you'd be here. I've walked past your cousin's apartment a dozen times but didn't know if you wanted to see me," he said.

"Of course I did. I always wondered what happened to you," I said.

A dark-skinned man approached us and asked, "Charles, you ready to go?"

"Yeah, I am. Um...Miss Mae, this is my friend, Fred," Charles said as Fred reached out his hand for me to shake.

I shook his hand. "Pleasure to meet you, Fred."

"Pleasure is all mine Miss Mae. You sounded beautiful up there," Fred said.

"Thank you," I replied, blushing.

Vivian walked up to us and wrapped her arms around my waist. She started talking about how great of a singer I was and how I should be the permanent singer at *Buck's*. The whole time she spoke I noticed that Fred never took his eyes off her. Who could blame him? Vivian was gorgeous. She had smooth, caramel skin. She carried herself with a regal elegance. Even as kids I always admired Vivian. She was perfection. So, I didn't blame Fred at all for being captivated by her.

When Vivian finished talking, Charles looked at me and said, "Miss Mae, would it be alright if I come check on you tomorrow?"

I smiled at him. "I'd like that. Thank you."

Then he and Fred said their goodbyes and left. I couldn't help but to watch as Charles walked away. His stride was confident and strong.

"Mmmm, that man is sweet on you, Mae," Vivian said.

"Who, Charles? No. He just feels obligated because of what happened with Uncle Buck, that's all," I said.

"Girl, tell yourself what you want," Viv said, not buying my reasoning. "I know men and that man is sweet on you."

"Oh, you know men? Then you know his friend seemed to be sweet on you, too," I teased her.

"Well, of course I saw that, but he ain't my type," she said.

I laughed. "What? Good looking ain't your type?"

"No, smart ass. The good boys. You know, the ones that want to rush you to the altar and have you popping out babies. That's who he is. I could smell him a mile away, and that ain't my type. I'd rather stay single and free, thank you very much," Vivian explained.

As she walked away I thought about what she said about Charles and wondered if she was right. Could someone as magnificent as Charles be interested in me? He was one of the good boys, as Vivian liked to call them. But that didn't bother me one bit.

Watch Over Me

That next day Charles came to visit after he got off work. He came the day after that and the next day, too. He even stopped calling me Miss Mae and started calling me Mae. Sometimes, when he felt like he was being funny, he'd call me Mrs. Dupuy. But the joke was on him because I rather liked being referred to as Mrs. Dupuy.

I started to sing twice a week at *Buck's* and Charles was always right there, in the front row. He would come by to see me while I worked in the shop with Mr. Polamo. He and Mr. Polamo even became the best of friends. They talked about everything from sports to current events. Mr. Polamo told Charles not to let them take him to that disgusting war that was going on. He even offered to hide Charles if need be. Prior to their conversation, it hadn't even occurred to me that Charles may leave me to go off to war. Of course, I should have thought about it. It seemed like all the men were leaving, but for some reason, I never thought Charles would be one of them.

Late one afternoon as we walked hand-in-hand in the park I asked him about it. I wanted to know if he thought he might have to leave.

"They're pulling people off the streets to go to 'Nam. A lot of the guys on the railroad have already gone and not by choice," he said.

"So, what you're saying is you may have to go?" I asked.

"No, Mae. What I'm saying is I don't know. I don't plan on fighting no losing war, especially the white man's losing war. But it seems like we ain't got no choice. They got this draft thing going and I don't really know how it works. All I know is a man gets called up and he don't come back," he explained.

I didn't want Charles to go. I didn't want him to leave me. He'd become my best friend. I shared everything in my head and heart with him. He made me feel safe and protected.

Charles stopped walking and held me in his arms. I held on to him for dear life. He was my anchor. Everything I was and would be was all wrapped in him. Vivian may have thought that the best thing Uncle Buck ever did was to give us that money. But the best thing he ever did for me was to have Charles bring me to New York.

I cried in his arms as if he was suited up, ready to deploy. Charles held me tighter and kissed me gently on the cheek. "No matter what, Mae, I'll always come back to you."

That made me cry harder. I didn't want him to come back because I never wanted him to have to leave.

✳✳✳

Later that night I had to sing at *Buck's*. The crowd had started to dwindle because so many men were off to war and women were working to support their families. But Vivian was convinced that *Buck's* would be the next big hot spot, so she hung on. I noticed she was drinking a little bit more than usual. I wasn't the only one who noticed. While Charles was backstage watching me get ready, Fred came in looking concerned.

"What's wrong?" I asked him.

"Viv's out there tossing them back with some gangster looking guys," he said. "I tried to tell her to take it easy, but she yelled at me to get away and said that what she does is none of my concern."

I ran and peeked through the curtains and saw the men Fred told us about. I'd seen them in *Buck's* a few times and I'd even seen Vivian leave with them on occasions. I figured she was dating one of them, but the last thing I wanted to do was tell Fred. He'd fallen hopelessly in love with Vivian, but she didn't seem to return the feelings.

"I think she's alright, Fred. Viv can handle herself," I said, trying to console him.

"It ain't about handling herself, Mae. Those guys mean her no good," he said.

"She's a grown woman, Fred. You can't force her into anything," I replied.

"Yeah, I guess." Fred walked back out to the front of the club.

Charles looked at me and shrugged his shoulders. I'd already told Charles about my concerns for Vivian and he'd had some of his own. But we both knew that Vivian had a lot of her daddy in her and she wouldn't be stopped, no matter what.

After I sang I joined Charles and Fred at their table. As we talked and laughed a man came up to us. I'd never seen him before. He was a short, white man with messy, brown hair and a shaggy beard. He was definitely out of his element at a club meant for Negros.

"Ms. Dupuy," he said.

"Yes?"

"I'm Elton St. John. I own a small record company and would love to bring you on board," he said.

"A record company?" Charles said, immediately suspicious.

"Yes, sir. Now, we're still growing, but with talent like yours I have no doubt that I can make you a star," he told me.

The word star danced around in my head and my face lit up. I looked over at Fred and Charles but they seemed far from convinced. Charles put his arm around me, letting Mr. St. John know that I was his. Then he said, "She'll think about it and get back to you."

The man handed me his card and walked off. I watched him leave and turned my attention to Charles.

"What did you do that for?" I asked. "That was the break I came to New York for!"

"That man could be playing you, Mae," Charles said.

Fred nodded in agreement. "He's right, Mae."

"He didn't seem like he was playing me. He seemed genuine," I told them.

"Come on, Mae. You've been here long enough to know how the game goes. This is a hustle," Charles said.

"I don't think it is," I said, insulted that he didn't think I was good enough for a record company to be genuinely interested in me. This was the first time Charles and I had ever disagreed and I didn't like it one bit. It seemed to me like he was trying to tell me what to do and I wasn't about to let that happen. I rose from the table, picking up Mr. St. John's card, and walked away. I decided I was going to be a big star like Mr. St. John said whether Charles liked it or not.

As it turned out, Charles definitely did not like it. When I made the appointment to meet Mr. St. John at his music studio, Charles took the day off from work to come with me. The studio wasn't close, but Charles got us there in that old pick-up truck of his.

Mr. St. John greeted us with hugs. His joy over our arrival made Charles even more suspicious, but I just ignored him. I happily followed Mr. St. John into a small room. There was a microphone standing behind a wall of windows, and a young, white man sat in front of a table full of knobs and buttons and lights. Mr. St. John introduce the man as Ben, his engineer. Ben shook our hands and then Mr. St. John asked me to go into the room with the microphone.

"Sing the Ella song," he instructed.

I walked up to the microphone and placed a set of headphones on my ears. The background music started to play and I began to sing. I got halfway through the song when the music turned off and Mr. St. John asked me to come back out. Ben played with a couple of the buttons on the table. Then I heard my voice fill the room. It was like magic. I sounded incredible. Even Charles had to smile as we listened. I sounded like a real singer. Not the little girl from a small, country town. I sounded like a star.

Mr. St. John jumped around, nodding his head. "Yes! This is the sound I want!" He walked up to me and put his hands on my shoulders. "Mae, I'm going to make you the next Ella."

"Really?" I said, smiling at him.

"Absolutely," he said. He let go of me and paced around the room. "We need to get you some songwriters. All we need is that one song that's going to put you on the map."

I turned and looked at Charles who finally seemed to be coming around. He originally thought this was just a hustle, but Mr. St. John hadn't asked me for money and he didn't seem to be working some kind of an angle. Even Charles had to admit this may be my big break.

NO!

It had been a few months since I started singing with Mr. St. John, but all the songs that he had written for me didn't seem to work. I was so scared that he would change his mind about me and decide that I was not worth the trouble. Every time I stepped into the booth Charles told me that something special was going to happen. But when I sang into that microphone nothing worked. Mr. St. John seemed to be getting more and more nervous. He was always pacing and growing angry when the songs didn't come out as he'd hoped.

One day when he angrily walked out of the room, I asked Ben what was wrong. "These studio sessions aren't cheap," he said. "And he owes a lot of money to some not-so-nice men. This has to work."

I felt even worse. Mr. St. John had been nothing but nice to me and now I was costing him money because I just couldn't get it right.

That night when I got home I ran into Fred standing outside of our apartment waiting on Vivian. This was a new habit he'd picked up because he felt like she was running with a rough crowd and needed his help. Truth was, *Buck's* was losing money and Vivian had blown through all the money that Uncle Buck had left her. Now she was running around drinking and partying.

"Hey, Fred," I said to him.

"Hey, Mae," he greeted me with a hug.

"Viv still ain't home yet?" I asked.

"No, not yet." He looked around, hoping that she would somehow appear. Then he noticed the concern on my face. "What's wrong, Mae?' he asked.

"I think I'm done singing before I even got started," I said.

"What do you mean by that?" Fred asked.

I sighed. "I can't seem to find a hit song."

"Well, Mae, it seems to me that hit songs come from somewhere deep within you. You got all these people writing a song for you, but they don't even know you," Fred explained.

"So, you're saying I should write my own song?" I asked.

"Maybe. Or maybe you can use this." Fred pulled out a folded piece of paper from his jacket pocket and handed it to me. "I wrote this for Vivian, but I know she's never going to read it. Besides, I think we both feel the same type of love. Maybe it'll do you more good than it did me." Fred hugged me goodbye and walked away.

When I got into my apartment I unfolded the paper and read the most beautiful love letter. It said exactly what I felt about Charles. I cried as I read every word. I didn't even have to get to the end to know that this was going to be my song. I would sing this for Charles and maybe Vivian would hear it and know just how much Fred loves her, too.

The next day I had Charles take me to Mr. St. John's studio. I told Mr. St. John and Ben that I had the perfect song, so they sent me back into the booth with the headphones playing. The beat started along with soft piano. And just when the tempo was about to pick up I looked into those perfect hazel eyes and I sang.

When I finished I looked at Mr. St. John and waited for a response but there was none. Both Ben and Charles were smiling and giving me the thumbs up, but Mr. St. John stayed silent. Then, fast as a lightning bolt, he ran into the booth. He flung his arms around me and picked me up off the ground.

"You did it, Mae! You did it!" he yelled as Charles and Ben laughed and hi-fived each other.

Mr. St. John pulled me out of the booth and had Ben replay the song. As I listened I held on to Charles. He kissed my forehead. I finally had my song.

✳✳✳

Two days later Mr. St. John asked me to come to the studio. Charles was working, so I went alone. When I got there, Mr. St. John was there with another white man who wore a tailored suit and sat with his legs crossed as he smoked a cigar.

"Mae," Mr. St. John said when I walked into the room.

"I came as soon as I could," I said nervously.

"You're fine, right on time," Mr. St. John said looking about as nervous as I felt. "I'd like for you to meet my business partner. This is-"

"No need for names," the man interrupted as he stood up to shake my hand.

"Yes, right. Sorry, sir." Mr. St. John was definitely nervous.

The man held on tightly to my hand with both of his. I could feel the heat of the cigar smoke as it landed on my skin. I was too nervous to pull my hand away. I looked into his blue eyes. There was something about this man I did not trust. Mr. St. John's fidgeting did nothing to ease my mind.

"I heard your song, Mae, and loved it," he said. "I'm prepared to put big money behind you." He finally released my hand and guided me towards a chair in front of Mr. St. John's desk.

"Yes. Mae is a talent," Mr. St. John said.

"That she is. With the recent upsurge of Negro music I think you can make me…us a lot of money," the man continued.

"Thank you," I whispered.

"Are you ready to be a big star?" he asked, leaning in close to me.

"Yes," I said quietly.

The man let out a loud laugh. "Good, good."

I sat there for a while as Mr. St. John and the man talked about how they were going to sell my song, which radio station they were going to send it to, how I should dress, and all kinds of other things that I didn't understand.

When they were finished they said I could leave. By then it was already dark and pretty cold outside. I stood on the side of the street waiting for a cab but none stopped. Just then the man came out of the building and a long black limousine pulled up in front of me.

The man stood beside me and said, "Well, I can't have my star standing in the cold, now can I?" He opened the back door of the limousine and motioned for me to get in. Something inside of me told me not to get in. I looked around hoping to see the familiar pick-up truck come around the corner, but it didn't. I didn't think I could refuse. So, I got in.

The limousine started moving and the man made himself more comfortable. He took off his jacket and loosened his tie. I sat staring straight ahead looking at the dark black walls inside the limo. I couldn't even see who was driving the car. The man poured some liquor into a glass and handed it to me. I told him I didn't drink and he found that funny. He drank the liquor himself while I sat perfectly still. I found it odd that he didn't even ask me where I was going or where I wanted to be dropped off.

"Mae, do you know what has made me a wealthy man?" he asked.

"No," I responded without looking in his direction.

"Because when I see what I want I go after it. The world belongs to me," he explained, putting down the glass and moving closer to me. "How big of a star do you want to be, Mae?" His hand slowly ran up my thigh and under my dress. I pushed it away but he kept going. "Tell me. How big of a star do you want to be?"

By that time his body was pushed against mine and his other hand was feeling on my breast. I didn't say a word. I tried to push him off me but he kept pinning me down.

"Oh, you're one of those nigger whores who likes it rough," he said.

He slapped me across my face and pulled me down on the seat. He ripped the top of my dress to expose my bra. Then he pushed up my dress and ripped off my panties.

"NO! NO!" I yelled. Tears streamed down my face and my body shook with fear. I wanted to jump out of the moving car but he pinned both my hands behind my back. I tried to kick him off but I could barely move under the weight of his body.

Then he was inside of me. My body jerked with every painful thrust. My screams were silenced by his hand crushing my mouth.

When he finished he got off me, smiling the same smile that was on the faces of the men who killed my uncle. I was paralyzed.

He pulled up his pants and then called for his driver to stop the car. When the car stopped the man opened the door and pushed me out, flinging my purse after me.

I sat on the sidewalk as the limousine drove off. I didn't know where I was. No one was on the streets. It was the first time since being in New York that no one was around.

I slowly stood up and tried to fix my dress, but somehow it didn't cover my bra anymore. It was ripped. Suddenly, I saw a cab coming and I signaled for it to stop. The cab driver noticed my appearance.

"Ma'am, are you alright? Would you like for me to take you to a hospital?" I shook my head no and gave him my address. I curled up in a ball in the back of the cab and stayed that way the entire ride home.

When we arrived at my apartment the cab driver asked again, "Are you sure you don't want me to take you to a hospital? You're bleeding, ma'am."

I looked down and saw the bottom of my dress was soaked with blood. I again shook my head no. I tried to pay him but he refused to take my money. I got out of the cab and immediately ran into Mr. Polamo closing up for the night. I fell into his arms, sobbing.

"Oh, Bella! What has happened to you?' Mr. Polamo asked. He called for his wife.

They put me in their car and drove me to their house. Mrs. Polamo took care of me. She removed my ripped, blood soaked dress and threw it in the trash. She drew a bath and helped me into the tub. She washed my back and brushed my hair as I sat in the tub of hot water, hugging my knees and sobbing.

When I finished bathing she gave me a nightgown and helped me lie down in bed. Then she knelt down by the bed and prayed in Italian. After she ended her prayer, she gave me a kiss on the forehead and walked out of the room, closing the door behind her.

A few moments later the door opened again. I slowly rolled over to see who had entered. Two perfect hazel eyes were looking back at me. I sat up. Charles rushed to me and held me in his arms as I cried.

What Now?

For days I stayed in the Polamos' spare bedroom. I couldn't eat. I couldn't speak. I could still feel that man on me. I couldn't get rid of the scent of cigar and liquor. I smelled it every time I took a breath. Charles never left my side. I feared he would be fired from his job, but that didn't seem to be a concern for him. He made sure he was there to wipe my tears every time I cried and to hold me when I started to shake. Having him with me gave me the strength to pull myself together and get out of bed.

One evening while Charles sat in the kitchen with Mr. and Mrs. Polamo, I walked into the kitchen and announced, "I'm ready to go home."

Charles stood, came over to me and held my hand. Mrs. Polamo came over and hugged me. I knew it was time to face the world again. It was time to get my life back and I could not do that locked away in a dark room.

That next morning Charles took me home to my apartment. Waiting for me was Vivian, arms outstretched. "Oh my God! Mae, I've been worried sick," she said. "Your Mama's been calling that payphone like crazy!"

"You didn't say anything…" The thought of Mama and Daddy knowing what happened to me sent me into a panic.

"No, no, don't worry. I didn't say a thing. I just told her you've been working on your music. She said she can't wait to hear it," Vivian said as she stroked my hair to calm me down.

"Oh, thank you," I said walking over to sit down on my bed.

Charles knelt down before me. "Alright now, Mae, I need to get to work but I'll be back right after. Mrs. Polamo will be coming up to check on you during the day."

"And I'll be here, too, Mae," Vivian added.

I gave Charles a hug goodbye and laid down on the bed. Vivian laid on her bed and stared at me. I realized this might be the first time in a long time that Vivian was sober.

"I'm sorry, Mae," she said.

"For what?" I asked.

"For not being there for you."

"What happened wasn't your fault, Viv."

"Maybe not, but you came up here because you trusted that I would take care of you and I didn't. There was just so much happening. I'm just really sorry, Mae," she said.

"I'm not mad at you, Viv," I assured her. "I'm mad at me."

"What do you mean?" she asked.

"I came here chasing some dream that wasn't meant to be. Guess I learned my lesson," I told her.

"No, Mae. Don't let this stop you. You're a great singer. Don't let him take that from you," Vivian pleaded.

"You know, Uncle Buck said I should go where God leads me, but I don't know where He's taking me. I don't know where I should go. What now? What am I supposed to do?" I asked.

It had been almost a month since that night. Everyone who knew called it 'the incident.' I guess no one wanted to say the word rape out loud. I guess no one wanted to remind me. I guess they thought I would forget and everything would be like new.

My mind tried to forget. The smell of cigar and liquor slowly faded away and I could no longer feel his touch all over me. But for some strange reason, my body didn't want to forget. I kept getting sicker and sicker. Every time I tried to stand up I felt lightheaded and nearly passed out. Mrs. Polamo would put cold towels on my head to keep my fever down. But when I started vomiting everything I ate, she insisted that I go to the hospital.

Vivian took me, and Charles met us there. I went in to meet with the doctor who examined me and asked me all kinds of questions. I didn't tell him about the incident and I didn't intend to. I didn't want anyone else to know. I couldn't face anyone else knowing.

When the examination was complete, I waited in the doctor's office with Vivian and Charles. I was scared of what the doctor was going to say. Maybe he would say I was dying or had some awful disease. But when he walked into the room and saw Charles holding my hand he put a smile on his face.

"Well, you didn't tell me your husband would be joining us," the doctor said.

The three of us looked at each other and silently came to the same conclusion that this white man need not know that Charles and I were not married. At least not until we heard what he had to say.

"I think congratulations are in order for you both," the doctor said.

"You do?" Charles asked.

"I mean you're pregnant. You two are going to have a baby," the doctor said, grinning.

I collapsed in Charles' arms and sobbed. Charles held me tight and whispered in my ear "It's going to be alright."

The doctor was confused by our reaction. Even Vivian was teary. There was no way to explain to him that this was not good news, that this baby was conceived on the worst night of my life. How was I going to forget the incident if I had to carry around that man's baby?

Unwanted Problems

For days I tried to forget about the pregnancy, and if it wasn't for the constant vomiting I think I could have. But my body kept reminding me that I was carrying the seed of a man that I wished was dead. A man who hurt me worse than anybody ever could. I wanted it to be over, but for the rest of my life I would be reminded of that night. I didn't know how I would cope. Mrs. Polamo just kept saying "Bella, God hasa plans. Faith, yes."

I couldn't imagine that God's plans for me would be to have the baby of the man who raped me. How would that be right? No one should have to do that.

Vivian woke up and got dressed one morning and said she had a plan for handling my circumstance. She told me to meet her later at *Buck's*. Vivian's idea of handling things weren't always my idea. But if she knew how to help me, then I was all in.

Later that day Charles, Fred and I met Vivian at *Buck's*. They insisted on coming because they didn't trust her plan either. When we arrived, Vivian was sitting at a bar with a white man dressed in a dark brown suit and a brown hat. She was surprised to see Charles and Fred.

"Oh, why did you bring them, Mae?" Vivian complained.

"Because we want to make sure you don't talk her into doing something crazy," Fred said.

Vivian looked insulted and propped a hand on her hip. "I would never do that to my cousin, Fred."

"It's ok. Who is this?" I asked, pointing at the man.

"This is Dr. Philips. He helped some of my friends get rid of unwanted problems, if you know what I mean," Vivian said with a wink.

Dr. Philips stood up and came over to shake my hand. I wasn't too keen on another white man touching me just yet. I pulled away and Charles offered his hand instead.

"Why are we meeting here and not your office?" Charles asked.

"Well, I like to go where my patients are. Besides, as you well know, this procedure isn't exactly legal," he explained.

"How much?" Fred asked as he folded his arms and gave the doctor a skeptical look.

"About a thousand," Dr. Philips said.

"A thousand dollars! We ain't got that kind of money, Doc," Charles said.

"Yes, Mae does," Vivian said glancing at me.

She knew that I had not spent one cent of the money that Uncle Buck gave me, but we promised not to tell anyone we had it. I had never even told Charles.

"Where is Mae gonna get that kind of money?" Charles asked.

Neither I nor Vivian wanted to say anything. We stood there looking at each other. I knew I had the money but if I spent it then everyone else would know too. Besides, I had vowed never to spend the blood money. But maybe the time was right.

"I have the money," I said softly.

"Where would you get that kind of money?" Charles asked.

I pulled Charles to the side and said to him, "You remember why my uncle died?"

"Yeah," he nodded, "he was in too deep with some white men."

"Well, I have that money. He gave it to me," I said to him.

Charles looked at me in disbelief. He was disappointed in me for keeping such a secret from him. I was disappointed in myself. The last thing I ever wanted to do was lie to Charles but I barely knew him when Vivian and I decided to keep this secret. I prayed he would understand.

"Please don't be mad," I said to him.

"I'm not Mae. How much more of it do you have left?" Charles asked, his face expressionless.

"All of it. I didn't want to spend it. Not after how they killed Uncle Buck. I couldn't live with myself," I said.

Charles smiled, looking relieved. He kissed the back of my hand and said, "Don't spend it now, Mae. Not for this."

"But what am I going to do Charles?" I asked in a panic. "I can't have this baby."

"You're going to trust me, Mae. We can handle this together."

"But how?"

"We were already talking about getting married, so let's do that now. No one outside the four of us and the Polamos will have to know that this ain't my baby. Mae, do you love me?" Charles looked at me with those hazel eyes and just like when we were in that old pick-up truck headed to New York, I knew that he would take care of me.

"More than anything," I replied.

"Then that settles it." Charles turned around and said to Dr. Philips, "Doc, we won't be needing your services."

Fred was happy but Vivian was so mad I could see steam about to come out of both her ears. Dr. Philips tipped his hat and left. Vivian couldn't believe the decision I'd made. I knew what she was thinking because I was thinking the same thing. There's no way I could have this baby, not even if Charles and I got married.

Star No More

Mr. And Mrs. Polamo were over the moon with excitement that Charles and I were getting married. They insisted that we have the wedding at their house. Charles and Mr. Polamo took care of all the arrangements and all I had to do was show up. Vivian was my maid of honor, Fred was Charles' best man, and the Polamos were our witnesses. Mrs. Polamo gave me her old wedding dress to wear. It was long, white lace with long sleeves and a high neck. Everything was so beautiful and all I could think about was that I was marrying the man God made for me.

Walking to Charles through the Polamos' living room as he stood next to the Justice of the Peace felt magical. For a moment, it was as though we were the only two people in the room. We were it. We were all we needed in the world. Nothing else mattered but the two of us.

I could hear the Justice talking, but all I saw were those perfect hazel eyes. Charles had spent almost all of his salary on the most beautiful wedding ring. I cried as he placed it on my finger. Knowing that I belonged to someone for the rest of my life was one of the best feelings in the world. I was his and he was mine.

After the ceremony, Mrs. Polamo brought out a cake that she had made from scratch. Charles and I cut it and fed it to each other. Then Fred asked, "Are you guys going to have your first dance?"

"What would we dance to?" I asked.

"How about this," Fred said, uncovering a vinyl record that he had hidden under a coat on the Polamos' couch.

"What's this?" I asked.

Fred handed the record over to me. "It's your song."

I couldn't believe it. "How did you get it?"

"Well, I met up with Mr. St. John who said since I wrote it I apparently owned it. He gave it to me. He also wanted to let you know that…you know…he was sorry and all," Fred said.

I stared at that record with so many mixed emotions. It was supposed to be the song that made me a star but now I was nowhere near being a star. Should I celebrate? Or should I throw this record away and never think of it again? I didn't get a chance to decide before Charles took it from my hand, and placed it on the Polamos' record player. The song started to play. Charles gently grabbed my hand and pulled me close to him. He held me tightly in his arms and all my fears subsided. We danced around that room as if we were floating on air.

The rest of the night was probably the best time I had since coming to New York. We laughed, we ate, and we drank. Mr. Polamo showed us how to celebrate Italian style. Even Vivian danced with Fred. It was an amazing night. I could not stop staring at Charles. He was absolutely mesmerizing.

While the others were in the living room talking and dancing, Vivian and I went into the kitchen to gather more food. I caught Vivian peeping around the corner to get a look at Fred. I chuckled.

"For someone who doesn't care about him you sho' act like you do," I said to her with a smile.

"I don't care nothing about him. Just wanted to see what was going on," she said and walked back over to where I was standing.

"Sure you did," I said with a giggle. "You know, he wrote that song for you."

"Who says?" she asked.

"That's what he told me," I said. "It was supposed to be a love letter for you."

"Yeah, well I don't believe that. Fred has a way of not telling the whole story," she replied.

"What do you mean by that? Fred's a good honest man," I said to her.

"If he's so honest then why didn't he tell you what really happened with that Mr. St. John?"

I didn't understand. "What are you talking about Viv? He did."

"Oh no, he didn't," she said, shaking her head. "It wasn't just him who went down to see that Mr. St. John. It was him and Charles. And they ain't go down there for no record either. Mr. St. John gave it to him so they'll leave him alone."

"What are you saying?" I asked, still not fully understanding.

"I'm saying they went down there to rough Mr. St. John up a bit," she clarified. "They thought he had something to do with what happened to you. Mr. St. John said he had no clue, but they didn't believe him. Charles was about to break his jaw when that other fella that works with Mr. St. John convinced them it was true."

"I...I don't believe you," I said to her. Vivian had been drinking and she could get a bit free with her mouth when some liquor get into her. I didn't know if her account of what happened was the truth or if she was talking just to be saying something.

"Fine, don't believe me. But that's what happened." She took a big sip of her drink.

"But why wouldn't Charles just tell me that?" I asked.

"Because then they'd have to tell you what happened next," Vivian said, taking another sip.

"What happened next?" I asked.

"Well," Vivian said, finally putting down her glass. "That devil man who hurt you was some kind of a banker and he was supposed to be taking money from the mafia and making it clean, but he was using it for his own personal use. Nobody but Mr. St. John knew about it. Well, after Charles and Fred worked him over and he heard what happened to you, Mr. St. John got chatty and told them mafia folks what that man been up to with their money. And now he's sleeping with the fishes!" Vivian burst into laughter and picked up her glass again.

"What does sleeping with the fishes mean?" I asked.

"Oh, Mae," she said, sitting her glass down again and grabbing my shoulders to look me in the eye. "It means he's dead. Your devil is dead."

I couldn't believe it. I had spent weeks in constant fear of this man, worried that I would be walking down the street and that long limousine would pull up beside me, snatch me inside and I'd have to relive that horrible night. But now that wasn't a possibility. He couldn't hurt me anymore. My hand brushed across my stomach and landed on my growing belly. For the first time that night I was reminded that he had left me with something that would ensure that he would be with me for the rest of my life. Even in death, he would haunt me.

Our wedding night was scary for me. Mr. and Mrs. Polamo paid for us to stay the night in a hotel. I wanted to be a wife to Charles and share my body with him. But I didn't know if I could handle the touch of a man. When we got into the hotel room Charles cupped my face in his hands. "It's ok if you're not ready."

"I want to be a wife to you, Charles." I said.

He smiled. "You already are, Mae."

He took my hand, led me to the bed and held me in his arms. I'd never felt so safe and so secure in my life. Laying there in Charles' arms I knew that he would never hurt me. I kissed my love. And that night, I allowed him to make love to me for the first time.

Want My Mama

After the wedding, Charles and I got an apartment next to Vivian's. Charles thought it would be easier for me to continue to be able to walk downstairs to work in the store with Mr. Polamo. He also figured that being close to Vivian meant she would be able to help me when he's not around. He figured wrong. Vivian slept all day and partied at *Buck's* all night. Vivian said that *Buck's* was hitting its sweet spot again. But to let Fred tell it, *Buck's* stopped being a classy joint and started being the go-to spot for local gangsters. I thought gangsters had been going to *Buck's* since it opened. But Fred convinced himself and Charles that it was now the worst juke-joint in New York City.

Vivian didn't care. The money was rolling in again and that's all that mattered. She flaunted around town in her mink coats and fancy dresses and hats. She even went shopping for the baby, buying toys, blankets, and bottles. I didn't even know where to put it all. Charles didn't care for it much. He said it was all bought with bad money. Vivian bragged that she tripled the money Uncle Buck left her. I was still holding on to mine, hiding it from Lord knows who.

Sometimes I worried about Vivian. Her drinking was getting worse, but Charles said I shouldn't worry because it was the life she chose. Besides, he hated it when I stayed up all night waiting for Vivian to get home. He said it was no good for the baby. But I just had to make sure she at least made it up the stairs and into her bed. I had to take care of Vivian. It felt like I was the only family she had left.

When Charles and I called Mama to tell her we had gotten married, Daddy was right there listening. He didn't like what he heard one bit. He took the phone from Mama and hung it up. I hadn't heard from them in weeks. I tried calling Mama, but when she picked up the phone and heard my voice, she'd hang up. I didn't even tell them about the baby.

On one of the rare occasions when Vivian was awake during the day, she came into my apartment and saw me sitting all alone, deep in thought. She sat down next to me. "What's wrong, Mae?"

"I really want my Mama," I said, my eyes filled with tears.

I didn't know what it meant to be married or to be someone's mother. I needed Mama to talk me through it all. But I didn't have her and I felt so lost and alone. Vivian took one look at me and then stormed out of the room. A few minutes later I heard her call my name from down the hall. When I got to her she was on the payphone. She said through the receiver, "Mae has done good, Aunty. You would be proud of her. I know I am."

She paused and handed me the phone. On the other end, I heard my mother's voice. "Mae?"

"Mama," I whimpered.

"Yes, baby. Why don't you tell me all about my new son-in-law," she said softly.

I told her about Charles. I told her how we met, how we spent our time together. I told her about the wedding and the Polamos. When I was done she said, "Oh, Mae. I really wish I was there."

"I wish you were here, too, Mama," I said, wiping the tears from my face. "I know you would like Charles. He's such a good man."

"I'm sure he is, Mae. To hear Viv tell it, men don't get no better than Charles," Mama giggled.

"They really don't," I said touching my belly. The one thing I didn't tell her about was the incident. Charles said that no one had to know except the folks that already knew. But I wanted to break down and tell Mama.

I looked up into Vivian's face and I was sure she could tell what I was thinking because she slowly shook her head no.

"Mama?" I said, tentatively.

"Yes baby?"

"I have one more thing to tell you," I said.

"What's that?" she asked

"I'm pregnant," I said quickly. "Mama, please don't be mad. I'm so scared and I really need you."

"Hold on, baby, hold on," she said, then paused. "Are you saying you're about to be a mother?" she asked.

"Yes, ma'am," I said bending my head.

"Oh, Mae," she said as she started to cry.

"Mama, are you ok?" I asked.

"I waited for this a long time, Mae. I missed your wedding but, baby, I promise you I won't miss this," she said.

Every day after that Mama and I spoke on the phone, sometimes three times a day. Either she was calling me or I was calling her. I had to convince Charles to install a phone in our apartment just so I could talk to my mama without someone interrupting me. Mama told me what to do when I wasn't feeling well and she agreed with Charles that I shouldn't be waiting up late for Vivian.

I asked her once about what Daddy thought. She said that he just needed time to get used to everything. But I knew that this was the final straw. First I disobeyed him and left for New York, then I married a man he didn't know, and now I was pregnant. I gave up all hopes of Daddy ever forgiving me. But my Mama was right there for me and for that, I was thankful.

A Home for Us

After a while, I could barely see my feet. My stomach had grown so big and it hurt to stand for long periods of time. Mrs. Polamo came upstairs with food and helped me get around. She and my mother had started speaking on the phone and they decided together that I needed to stay in bed as often as possible. I was only allowed to get up to go down the hall to the bathroom when Mrs. Polamo came to check on me.

Vivian had grown tired of living in a cramped, one room studio and had moved into a big, lavish apartment a few blocks away. She'd thrown herself a big house warming party, but Charles and I couldn't go. Fred went and came right back to our apartment after about an hour. He said it wasn't his kind of scene. I could tell Fred was giving up all hopes of him and Vivian ever being together. He had started dating a young lady who worked as a nurse at the local hospital.

He brought her by a few times to have her check on me and to make sure the pregnancy was alright. I, too, had held out hope that he and Vivian would find their way to each other. But I had to admit that his new girlfriend, Sharon, was more his speed and a lot better for him. Vivian was too busy partying to realize that Fred had moved on from her.

She was loving her new apartment so much that she put it in Charles' head that our tiny apartment was no place to have a child. I could tell that Charles was growing uneasy because he and Mr. Polamo always seemed to have their heads together in discussion, and I suspected they were talking about us getting a new home.

One day Mr. and Mrs. Polamo came to our apartment and said that their nephew, Joey, had an old house close to where the Polamos' lived in Harlem. Mr. Polamo insisted that Charles go with him right then and there to see it. Mrs. Polamo refused to let me go. She said to let the men handle it while I stayed in bed.

A couple of hours later Charles and Mr. Polamo came back with big smiles on their faces. Charles came right over and gave me a hug. "Oh, Mae! It's incredible."

Charles' excitement was infectious. He described the new place to me. It was a basement apartment with two bedrooms and a bathroom. Above the basement was a whole house with a dining room, kitchen, living room, with bedrooms and bathrooms on the second floor. He said that the house itself wasn't done because it was being renovated and that's why Mr. Polamo's nephew was only renting out the basement apartment. But then Charles said that he and Mr. Polamo struck a deal with Joey, allowing Charles to fix up the house while we lived in the basement apartment. In exchange for paying him for the work, our rent would go towards buying the whole house.

"We could own it, Mae. It would be our home, a home for us. Isn't that amazing?" he said excitedly.

"That's incredible Charles, but when will you have time to fix an entire house?" I asked confused.

"I'll make time, Mae," he declared. "For our family, I'll make time."

I could see the determination in Charles' eyes. He was going to make this work so that we would have a home. It made me love him all the more.

***

About a week later we moved into our new home. The Polamo's helped us get a few dishes and household things. But Vivian showed up with a big moving van filled with bedroom and living room furniture. She furnished our entire apartment and even bought a crib for the baby. Of course, since she bought the furniture she made sure our new apartment was decorated just the way she liked.

Fred showed up to help and brought Sharon with him. It was the first time Vivian had seen or even heard of Sharon. I thought she was going to have a stroke when Fred walk through the door holding Sharon's hand. But when Fred held up Sharon's ring finger and announced that they were going to be married I thought for sure Vivian was going to attack the poor girl. She looked as though all the blood drained from her face. I guess you never know what you've got until it's gone. Vivian was feeling the sting of losing a good man, one who loved her beyond herself, and she didn't like it one bit.

Vivian spent the rest of the evening pretending to decorate, but the whole time she stared a hole in Sharon's head. I could see her taking mental notes of all that was wrong with Sharon just so she could bring it up later. I knew Vivian better than she knew herself and I've always known that her heart belonged to Fred. But she had too much of her daddy in her to ever settle down. She was both regretful and angry. She barely spoke to Fred and he did all he could not to look in her direction. The two of them were a mess. I felt sorry for Sharon because she was caught in the middle of a love that was complicated and made absolutely no sense.

After everyone left, Charles turned on an old record player he found and started to play my record. Then he grabbed me by the hand and we danced around. I never felt as safe or as loved as I did every time I was in Charles' arms.

✳✳✳

A few weeks had gone by and I was as big as a house. Charles had started working on the renovations upstairs whenever he had free time. Fred would often come by to help him out, but Charles was determined to finish the house, even if he had to do it all alone.

He was up there working alone when I went into labor. I took the broom and banged on the ceiling trying to get his attention. Charles came running down the stairs and rushed me to the hospital. When we got there we ran into Sharon, who made sure I was taken care of. She called Fred, and he called the Polamos' and Vivian, who somehow managed to be completely sober that night. When Vivian and the Polamos got to the hospital I was already in the delivery room, scared out of my mind and my body riddled with pain.

There were doctors and nurses around me wearing masks. They wouldn't allow Charles in the delivery room with me, but Sharon came in so I wouldn't feel alone.

Just when I thought I wouldn't be able to make it through, I heard the doctor say, "Ok, Mae. I see the head. Give me one big push."

Sharon and another nurse stood on opposite sides of my bed. They each grabbed one of my arms and helped me to sit up. I gripped my thighs and pushed that baby out with all of my strength. The doctor lifted the baby up so I could see it. "It's a boy!"

Sharon left my side and went to wrap the baby in a blue blanket. She laid him on my chest so I could get a better look at him. I turned to look at him and the first thing I saw were blue eyes staring back at me. The fear of that night came rushing back and I began to cry hysterically. All the doctors and nurses stopped what they were doing and looked at me. My doctor said, "I know, Mae. It's a bit overwhelming."

Sharon rubbed my arm and took the baby away. She came back over and said, "I'll take him to the nursery and let your family know. Don't worry, he'll be just fine."

As Sharon rolled the baby out the room I feared that I would never be able to look at him without seeing the man who hurt me. What if I'm never able to love him?

My Boy

Mama came up to visit with Franny a week after I came home from the hospital. She was so excited to see her first grandbaby that she didn't notice how I kept my distance from him.

"What's his name?" she asked, picking up the baby and rocking him in her arms.

"Charles, Jr," Charles announced, beaming with pride.

"Oh my Lord," she said smiling from ear to ear. "He is absolutely beautiful. Mae, you did a great job, baby. I'm so proud of you."

I smiled reluctantly, still unable to look at the baby. Franny was all over him like he was a little doll for her to play with. She had gotten so tall since the last time I saw her and I realized that I hadn't seen my family in over a year. I started to cry. Charles held me close and kissed my forehead.

"Oh, don't you pay her no mind, Charles. She's going to do that a lot. We women get all emotional around this time," Mama said with a smile.

I knew she had no idea what I was going through. She thought it was normal, new mother stuff. But it wasn't. Nothing about me having this baby was normal at all.

For the next few weeks, Mama and Mrs. Polamo did everything for me. Mama tried to show me how to feed and bathe the baby, but I didn't want to touch him. The one thing she didn't let me get away with was not breastfeeding. She said it was good for the baby and when I get out of my funk I would regret not doing it. The first couple of times I turned my head away from him as he latched on to my breast. My skin grew cold from his little puffs of breath. I was shaking and could barely hold him. I didn't want to.

Mrs. Polamo came over to me when my mother wasn't around and said "Bella, he's your boy, yes. Your boy."

But my mind couldn't wrap around that statement. Every time I looked at him all I saw was blue eyes. His blue eyes said he belonged to that man. He *was* that man. It had gotten so bad that at night I imagined I smelled cigars and liquor again.

For Charles, this was easy. When he looked at the baby all he saw was his son. Nothing else mattered to him. But I couldn't see that. I couldn't distinguish this baby from that man.

When Mama saw that I was having difficulties she decided to stay a little longer. She was the one who got up when the baby cried at night, changed his diaper, and fed him. I was completely useless to this baby.

One night I woke Charles from his sleep. "I think the baby should go with Mama when she leaves."

Charles sat up in bed and looked at me. "What are you talking about, Mae?" he asked.

"I can't offer him anything, Charles. I'm no good for him," I told him.

"He's our boy, Mae," he said. "He ain't going nowhere."

That was the first time he was ever stern with me. I knew that he would not let the baby go. But how could I let the baby stay? How would I be able to raise a child that I could barely look at? Charles laid back down and repeated, "He's our boy."

The next morning I woke up and the house was empty. It was just me and the baby. Mama left a note saying Mrs. Polamo had taken her and Franny to the store to get some groceries and I knew that Charles was already at work.

I sat in the living room, quietly praying the baby wouldn't wake up from his nap. I hoped that he could just sleep until Mama got back. But he started to cry. I sat still, hoping he would go back to sleep. But his cries grew louder. I sat on the edge of the sofa rocking back and forth, covering my ears. He started to scream. Then he began to cough as though he couldn't breathe.

I got up and went into the room and peered into his crib. His little body was shaking and he made sounds as though he was in distress. Fear crept through me and without thinking, I picked him up and held him close in my arms. I didn't know what to do. I ran outside and flagged down a cab. The cab driver took us to the closest hospital. The moment I walked into the emergency room I shouted, "My Boy! My Boy needs help!"

1966

Charlie was almost five and I never let him out of my sight. It's funny how I went from not wanting to hold him to never wanting him to leave my side. But after almost losing him the thought of being without my baby scared me. Even though the doctors said that he only had a cold and the mucus caused him to cough and struggle to breathe, it was still a close call for me. It was also too close for Mama. Even after she was back in North Carolina, she called every day just to talk to him and make sure he was alright. She made me hold the phone up to his ear and she would converse with him as if she was talking to a grown person. But he listened and laughed like he understood every single word she was saying.

Charlie was the light of all of our worlds. The Polamos spoiled him rotten and wanted to show him off. They made such a fuss over him in the store that customers sometimes thought he was their very own grandbaby. Hell, he was light enough to pass. It was a good time.

The only person who didn't seem all that happy was Charles. I could tell something was wrong with him because he seemed so down every time he came home from work. He was nearly finished with fixing the house upstairs. The only time his eyes sparkled was when he played with Charlie. There was definitely something going on and not knowing scared me.

One night I waited until he was done with his supper and was playing with Charlie. I sat down on the floor beside them and asked, "What's wrong, Charles?"

"What do you mean?" he asked.

"You seem so unhappy. Please tell me what's going on," I pleaded.

He shook his head. "I don't want you to worry, Mae."

"I worry when I don't know," I said.

"Ok," he said, looking up at me. "The fellas down on the railroad aren't happy and the union's talking about a strike."

"A strike? What does a strike mean?" I asked.

"It means no work and no work means no pay," he explained.

I was concerned. "But for how long?"

"For as long as it takes for them big bosses to change conditions," he said. "And who knows if they ever will."

"But what would we do for money?" I asked.

"That's why I didn't want to tell you, Mae. I can figure this out. I promise you I won't let you or Charlie down," Charles said as he grabbed my hand.

"I know you won't, Charles. But I don't want you to carry this all alone. We're a team now. Besides, I still have the money from Uncle Buck. We'll be alright," I said, trying to console him.

"No, you were right not to use that money. To make it clean we need to use it for something good. I don't think this is it," Charles said.

"What could be better than keeping food on the table?" I asked him.

"I don't know, Mae," he admitted, "but this ain't it. I'm a man and I'm gonna provide for this family, I promise you that."

But as the days went on it seemed the threat of a railroad strike loomed like a dark cloud overhead, and the stress weighed heavily on Charles. Then one day in the middle of the afternoon, Charles came home completely distraught. There was officially a railroad strike and Charles was out of work.

For days Charles tried to find work, but couldn't. He went everywhere asking about positions. But nothing came of his efforts. Fred was also out of work but Sharon managed to find him a job working in the hospital as a custodian. It was a night job but Fred didn't mind at all. He tried to get Charles a job working with him but nothing seemed to come his way.

When we were unable to make rent, Joey Polamo came around. He and Charles had struck up a friendship. So he tried, unsuccessfully, to find Charles a construction job.

One evening Mr. Polamo came to the house with a teddy bear for Charlie. He sat in the living room looking exhausted. Charles gave him a glass of wine and sat down beside him. I stayed in the kitchen tending to Charlie but still listened in on their conversation.

"Charles, I'm getting old," Mr. Polamo said.

"No, sir," Charles replied with a grin.

"Si, Si. No more young man. This I know. So you come work for me in the store. I need someone I trust," Mr. Polamo said.

"Do you mean it, sir?" Charles asked. "I mean, your family has been so great to us. I can't…"

"No. You're family too. So you come work for the family and run the store," Mr. Polamo said.

Charles was over the moon with excitement and so was I. Not only had he found a job but he was also going to be working with me. Most importantly, this could be something permanent, something that he could do for years to come. Mr. Polamo wanted to teach Charles how to run the store so that Charles could take over when he retired. This was exactly what we needed.

Charles began working in the store with Mr. Polamo the very next day. He took in every aspect of the store. He learned how to order supplies, how to stock the shelves, and price the merchandise. After a few months, Mr. Polamo was comfortable enough with Charles being in charge that he started spending more time at home and less at the store. Pretty soon, he barely came to the store at all.

Working at the Polamos' store revived Charles. He got back to work finishing our house until one day he burst into the apartment and shouted, "Mae! Mae! I'm done!" He scooped up Charlie, took me by the hand and led us up the stairs and into the house.

It was absolutely beautiful. I walked around and took it all in. The walls were freshly painted white, there were shining wood floors that led from the living room all the way to the dining room. The kitchen was big and beautiful and I hadn't even gone upstairs yet. I ran over to Charles and gave him a hug.

"You did it. I knew you could," I said to him.

"I promise you I'll take care of us. 1966 is turning out to be our year, Mae," he said.

"Yes, it is," I replied.

When God Calls Your Name

We were living upstairs in the house and loving it. Charlie was growing like a weed and kept me on my toes. Charles worked hard in the Polamos' store and had made it more profitable than it already was. Because Charles was black, more black folks started coming in and spending their money at the store.

Fred and Sharon were still engaged but never did get married. Charles used to tease Fred about having cold feet. But I knew the reason he couldn't marry Sharon was because he was still crazy about Vivian.

Vivian was all over the place. *Buck's* had closed down by then and we never really knew what she was doing. Somehow she still had the money to keep that lavish apartment of hers and all the mink coats and fancy clothes. Charles said the less we knew the better off we'd be. I had to agree because there was no telling what that girl was getting into. She had a lot of her daddy in her.

She would come around every now and then, looking like a million dollars. I wanted to ask her what she'd gotten herself into but I thought better of it. The last thing I wanted to concern myself with was all of Vivian's mess. I had my hands full with Charlie and I stopped working at the store so I could spend more time helping Mrs. Polamo take care of Mr. Polamo. His health was deteriorating and Mrs. Polamo could barely move around herself. I would take Charlie with me and clean up around their house and fix their meals. It was the least I could do after everything they had done for me.

All that helping I was doing didn't make much of a difference, especially when God calls your name. Before I arrived one morning, Mr. Polamo collapsed in the middle of the living room and couldn't be revived. Mrs. Polamo called for an ambulance, but by the time they arrived he was dead. I felt like I had lost my own father. Mr. Polamo took the father role in my life when my daddy wanted nothing to do with me. He was such a good man.

Mama came up for the funeral and brought Franny and Buddy with her. Buddy had never been to New York or even seen Charlie. I was so excited when they arrived. That was Mama's first time seeing the finished house and I couldn't wait to hear what she thought. I just knew she'd love it and she did. She gave Charles a huge hug and told him how proud she was of him for doing all that work. Buddy also seemed impressed with Charles. He followed Charles everywhere he went.

Mama and I helped Mrs. Polamo make the arrangements for the funeral while Buddy went to work with Charles at the store. Franny stayed at the house with Charlie. It was a tough couple of days for all of us but especially for Mrs. Polamo. She walked around as if she were lifeless. Mama said for a couple that's been together for as long as the Polamos had, it would be tough for Mrs. Polamo to function without her husband.

But Mrs. Polamo held on. Even through the funeral service she never shed a tear and never even got up to say goodbye to Mr. Polamo. I watched her and then stared at Charles. The thought of living on this earth without him scared me. I wouldn't be half as brave as Mrs. Polamo.

After the funeral, we went to the gravesite. Mrs. Polamo held on to my hand and asked me to sit beside her. She said I was family and I should sit where the family sat. I agreed so that I wouldn't upset her, but I felt uncomfortable sitting there among a sea of Italian folks. All of them looked at me like I made a wrong turn somewhere. But Mrs. Polamo held on to my hand and refused to let me go. So I didn't let her go either. I sat beside her as the casket was lowered into the ground. And then I held on to her as we slowly walked away. I asked her if she was going to be alright and she said, "Si, Bella. When love comes, it stays and no death can take it away."

I squeezed her hand and got with her into the car headed back to her house where a few family members and friends were waiting. Once she was seated and comfortable in the living room, I left her there with my mother and Charlie and went to find Charles. He was sitting outside talking with Joey. When Joey saw me he said, "Good. Since you both are here there's something I should tell you."

"What is it?" Charles asked.

Joey pulled out a piece of paper and handed it to Charles. "That's a copy of my uncle's will," he said. "He wanted the two of you to have the store."

"What?" I asked in disbelief.

"Yeah, he thought that you two worked hard enough for it so he wanted you to have it. He said you two were the closest thing to children that he had, so why not give it to you."

"But what about Mrs. Polamo?" I asked.

"She knows and is in perfect agreement," he assured me.

I could not believe our good fortune, and judging by Charles' face, neither could he. We had our very own store.

"Thank you, sir," Charles managed to say as he read over Mr. Polamo's will.

"Well, don't thank me just yet because there's more." Joey pulled out another piece of paper from his pocket and handed that over to Charles as well.

"That is the deed to the house," Joey said.

"What? No, sir. We still owe you." Charles looked at Joey, confused.

Joey pointed to a sentence in Mr. Polamo's will. "No, you don't. He paid it off. The house is yours."

"I…I don't know what to say." The shock and joy on Charles' face said enough.

I, too, was in shock. The Polamos had already done so much for us that I didn't need or expected anything else from them. I owed them beyond measure, yet they gave my family even more.

"Just say I can still come over and hang out," Joey said with a smile.

"Yes, anytime. You're more than welcome," Charles replied, shaking his hand.

✳✳✳

Once we got home, Charles and I told Mama what happened. She fell to her knees and thanked God. She embraced us, tears streaming down her face.

Mama, determined to pay Mrs. Polamo back for all her husband had done, decided to stay in New York a little while longer. Franny and Buddy were just fine with that because Franny liked being around Charlie and Buddy liked working with Charles in the store. Every morning

Mama got up and tended to Mrs. Polamo's house. She would stay there for hours, sometimes all day. Occasionally I would go with her to see Mrs. Polamo. She told me during one of my visits, "Bella, love never leaves you. It always finds you. Just wait until it comes back to get you."

A couple of weeks after Mr. Polamo died, love came back to get Mrs. Polamo. She went to sleep one night and never woke up. I pictured them up there in heaven, together again.

It's Vietnam, for God's Sake

The few years after Mr. and Mr. Polamo died were pretty quiet. Charles worked hard at the store. I dropped Charlie off at school and then joined Charles in the store until it was time to pick him up again. There was peaceful normalcy in our lives.

The war in Vietnam started to heat up even more and there was talk of sending more men off to fight. I used to sit around in the living room watching the news on TV, praying that no one came looking for my Charles. Night in and night out I prayed. Charles said I was just going to make myself crazy. He said they didn't even know he existed. "I was born in the swamp, in the bayous, Mae. Don't nobody even know I'm here."

"That don't mean nothing, Charles. They're the government. They know everything," I said to him.

"No ma'am," he said with a chuckled. "They don't know me. No records means you were never born. I don't even have a birth certificate. So, they can't come get me and I damn sure ain't about to go volunteer."

One day Joey came by the house while my eyes were glued to the TV. He walked in, saw me staring at the screen and laughed out loud. "That's exactly why I'm here," he said.

"What? They got you, too?" Charles asked.

"No. I'm not giving them a chance. I'm headed back to Italy for a while, at least until all this mess is over," he answered.

"What about all your businesses?" Charles asked.

"I'm taking measures to take care of that. I just wanted to stop by and tell you both goodbye." Joey stretched out his hand to Charles.

"We'll miss you," Charles said as he took Joey's hand in his own.

I stood up and gave Joey a hug. "Thank you for everything."

"No. Thank you guys for being so good to my aunt and uncle. I was just repaying the favor," Joey replied. "I'm sure we'll see each other soon."

Joey left and part of me wondered how easy it would be for us to go to Italy too. It would be the perfect place to go if Charles ever got drafted. Joey was smart to leave. I only wished Charles was as concerned as Joey.

Joey's leaving only further intensified my TV watching for war updates. For a white man like Joey to be so worried about being called to serve only meant that this was serious. Every day I picked up Charlie from school I hurried home to make sure I didn't miss anything.

One day Vivian came over. She was decked out, as usual, but her hair and makeup were messy.

"What's wrong with you?" I asked.

"Oh, nothing," she said, waving me off.

"Have you been drinking?" I noticed she was a little unsteady on her feet.

"No, Mae. I'm fine," she answered.

Something told me that Vivian was not fine. Her eyes were glassy and a little red. She was fidgety and uneasy. I watched her, trying to figure out what was going on. This made Vivian even more uneasy.

"Are you just going to keep looking at me?" she asked.

"You look different," I said.

But before I could figure out what was wrong with her, the front door opened and in walked Charles, followed by Fred dressed in a full army uniform. The sight sent shivers down my spine. Vivian's jaw almost hit the floor.

"Oh no," I said running over to hug Fred.

"Oh, Mae. Don't you do that. It will be alright," Fred said.

"Yeah, right," Vivian said with a snicker.

"It will be," he said, looking at her.

"But when will you leave?" I asked.

"I ship out in two days," he said. "Then I'll be back."

"No, you won't," Vivian said.

Fred looked at Vivian. "I will."

Vivian walked towards Fred. "Do you know how many men I know who have already gone and they ain't come back?"

"That's always been your problem, Viv. You always compare me to those other men you know. I've always been different and I will be back," he said.

"Men are all the same. Ain't no difference between them," she said. "It's Vietnam for God's sake! You ain't coming back!" Vivian stormed off, slamming the front door behind her. Fred looked distraught.

"She's just upset," I said to Fred, rubbing his arm.

"Yeah, you know how Viv gets," Charles added. "Why don't you tell Mae what else you wanted her to know?"

"Um…Sharon and I are getting married tomorrow morning. I would really like for you and Charles to be there. You guys are my family," Fred told me.

"Of course we'll be there," I said. "We wouldn't miss it for the world."

"Great. Um, I should go," Fred said, his voice heavy with sadness.

The next morning Charles, Charlie and I got dressed and met Fred and Sharon at the courthouse. Sharon seemed excited to finally become Fred's wife. But Fred seemed preoccupied. There was a hint of sadness in his face, almost like regret. He looked at Sharon as they stood in front of the Justice of the Peace almost as if he wished she was someone else. I knew who that someone was. But Sharon was so happy that I don't think she even realized that Fred's heart wasn't in it.

I wanted to stop the ceremony and yell at Fred to go after Vivian and not stop until she knows how much he loved her. I wanted him to know what it felt like to have the one person you love most in the world love you back. Vivian was right, he may not come back. How sad to think he may never be with the woman he loved before he died.

I was already killing this man off before he even stepped foot on the plane. Charles must have figured out what I was thinking because he grabbed my hand to hold me in place. I wanted to slap sense into Vivian. How could she deny this man her love? How could she deny herself his love?

The best part of me came alive the day I found Charles and I just knew that the best part of her would do the same if only she would let Fred love her. I guess our hearts do what they want to do. I could see how much Sharon loved Fred, but I could also see how much Fred longed to be loved by Vivian.

After the ceremony, we went back to our house to celebrate. Sharon was on cloud nine and I didn't want to do anything to disturb that. So I kept my mouth shut. Even when we went to see Fred off, I said nothing. I watched as Sharon kissed him goodbye and he looked around as if he expected Vivian to come running up to him. I said nothing.

✳✳✳

It had been over a month since Fred had gone and I hadn't seen Vivian that entire time. She hadn't called or popped up like she usually did. So, one Saturday I let Charlie go to work in the store with his father and I went to find Vivian.

There were pieces of paper taped to her apartment door. I took them down and then knock as hard as I could. She opened the door, looking like a wreck. I walked into her fancy apartment and it was absolutely disgusting. There was trash everywhere, all the furniture was gone and it smelled like something or someone had died.

"What happened to all of your things?" I asked her.

"I had to sell it all a couple of days ago," she replied. "But it wasn't enough anyway."

I looked around. "What did you need the money for?"

"To take care of a problem I have," she said.

"What kind of problem could you...oh," I said, stunned when I realized what she meant.

"Yes, Mae. I'm pregnant," she confirmed.

"Who is the father? One of the gangsters you always running around with?" I asked.

"No, Mae," she said, sitting on the floor with her legs crossed.

"Then who?" I asked.

Vivian took a long pause and announced, "Fred. Fred's the father."

"But…What?" I was confused. I was sure Vivian had lost what little was left of her mind.

"Do you remember the night he announced to us that he was leaving?" she asked.

I nodded. "Yes. I do."

"Well after he left your house he came over here and we talked. He told me how much he loved me and if I was so sure that he was not coming back then he felt like I should know," she explained.

I was shocked. I never knew that Fred did that. That he actually had the nerve to tell Vivian the one thing he'd been so afraid to say for so long. I felt proud of him in that moment.

"The two of you made love after that," I concluded.

"No one had said those things to me before," she confessed. "No man has ever thought I was that special, Mae. I just wanted to hold on to that feeling a little while longer."

"So, then why get rid of his baby, Viv?" I asked. "You have been blessed to have a baby that came from love. Keep this baby, Viv."

She grinned. "Can you picture me as somebody's mama, Mae?"

"Yes, I can. I think you'll make a great mama," I replied, giving her a hug.

"I don't have any money left, Fred's gone off to die, and I won't even have a place to live in a few days," she said.

"Why?" I asked.

She pointed at my hand. "All those papers you're holding are eviction notices. No money to pay my rent, Mae."

"So come home with me," I said.

"What? I can't," she said, shaking her head.

"Of course you can. My home is your home. Besides, no one lives downstairs in that basement apartment. It's just sitting there," I told her.

She thought for a moment. "But would Charles mind?"

"Of course he wouldn't," I said.

Two days later Vivian moved into the basement apartment. I made sure that she wrote Fred and told him about the baby. Fred wrote back expressing his excitement but asked that we not tell Sharon. He said that he would do that himself when he got back. I think a part of Fred figured he would come back, divorce Sharon and he, Vivian, and the baby would be a family. A little part of me hoped that it worked out that way because they both deserved it.

It's Drugs

Vivian had to go into the hospital because the baby was in trouble. The doctors were nervous that the baby was not going to make it, so they decided to deliver it early. I was allowed in the delivery room with Vivian. The doctors had to cut her open to take the baby out and she was scared. So was I. But when the doctor pulled out an adorable, chocolate, little girl, Vivian took one look at her and fell in love.

"She's beautiful, Mae," Vivian declared.

I smiled at her, "I know!"

The nurse took the baby, wrapped her in a pink blanket, and brought her over to Vivian. Vivian held the baby in her arms and ran her fingers lightly across the tiny face.

"Have you thought about what you want to name her?" the nurse asked.

"Domonique. Because she's unique. She's going to be better than me, Mae. You'll see," Vivian said.

✳✳✳

Vivian came back to our basement apartment after she had Domonique. For a while, Vivian was a completely different person. She wasn't focused on partying and money. It was all about Domonique. She even sent a few pictures to Fred and told him that she gave Domonique his last name. Vivian had hope again. The best part of her was wrapped in Domonique and for a while, it showed through.

But when Domonique was about eight months old and Fred had not come home yet, the part of Vivian that was more like her daddy started to come back. She started leaving Domonique with us as she went out at night, and she'd come back so drunk that she couldn't take care of Domonique at all during the next day.

I tried to tell her that she had to be a better mama, but she didn't want to hear it. "I need to make money, Mae. I can't be sitting here wasting my time. How can I be a good mama if I can't provide for her?" she would say to me.

But all that baby needed was her mama. Vivian was useless. I wanted her to stop drinking and take care of her daughter. Charles told me to let it go, that Vivian was just being who she was. He told me to bring Domonique's things upstairs and let her stay with us until Vivian got herself together.

I did so, but still tried to keep an eye on Vivian to convince her to be there for her daughter. Nothing seemed to get through to her. It was as if something had control over her, something that was stronger than the love for her own daughter. I couldn't imagine what that could be.

One day Charlie came in the house from playing outside and told me and Charles that he saw people coming in and out of Vivian's basement apartment. Charles ran down there to see what was going on. I left Domonique with Charlie and told him to lock the door behind me. I could hear Charles yelling for people to get out before he called the cops. Women and men ran out, looking like zombies. I made my way into the apartment. It looked as though there had been a party. Everything had been destroyed.

"Where's Vivian?' I asked.

Charles pointed towards the bedroom. Vivian was laying across the bed, almost naked and passed out. Something that looked like a rubber band was tied around her upper arm, and a needle was stuck inside her arm.

"What…What is that?" I asked

"It's drugs!' Charles yelled. "She brought drugs into our home!" He walked out and slammed the door to the apartment behind him.

I went over to the bed. I carefully took the needle out of Vivian's arm, untied the rubber band and threw them both in the trash. Then I went to the bathroom and filled the tub with water. I dragged Vivian to the bathtub, dumping her in the water. That woke her up. She splashed around in a panic.

When she realized that I was the one who put her there she screamed at the top of her lungs, "Mae, what are you doing?!"

"I'm trying to sober you up," I said to her.

Vivian sat up in the tub rubbing the water out her eyes. "I can't believe you did that," she said.

"I can't believe you brought all kinds of folks and drugs into my house! For God's sake, Viv, your daughter is right upstairs," I told her.

"Mae, will you grow up? This is 1970. Everyone parties like this. It's no big deal," she said.

"It is a big deal, Viv. You can't stay here like this," I told her.

"Then fine. I'll just get my baby and we'll leave." She started to climb out of the tub, wrapping a towel around herself.

"No you won't, Viv. I ain't letting you go nowhere with that baby," I told her.

"She's my baby, Mae. You can't stop me from taking her," Vivian said as she started to get dressed.

"Oh yes I can, Viv, and I will. If you want to live your life like this, then that's on you. But that child won't. I'ma keep her safe, even if it means from you. At least until Fred gets back," I told her.

"He ain't coming back, Mae!" she shouted. "When you gonna learn that?"

"Whether he comes back or not that child's not going anywhere with you!" I shouted back.

"Fine!" Vivian left and never looked back.

I wrote to Fred and told him what happened. I explained that Vivian was on drugs and there was no helping her. He wrote back and I could feel his pain on every page. I was heartbroken for Fred. I knew that he wanted to be with Vivian, but her demons would not allow that.

I watched Charlie as he tried to entertain Domonique. I wanted the best for them. I wanted them to have what Vivian and I didn't have. I felt like they deserved more.

The next morning I got up and left Charles with the kids. I made my way to the bank, clutching my brown pouch from Uncle Buck. Inside, I sat down with a white man in a business suit. I told him I had a lot of money that I wanted to invest. I said that I wanted it to grow. He helped me put it in something called an interest bearing savings account. He said that as long as I don't touch it, it would be more than enough money for the children. I laughed to myself because that man just didn't know how long I could go without touching that money.

I went back home, proud of myself. I sat Charles down and told him what I had done. A smile came across his face and he said, "I knew you'd figure out the right thing to do with that money. But are you sure it's going to be enough for the both of them?"

"Well, the man at the bank said that all three of them will have what that they need," I said.

Charles looked puzzled. "Three?"

"We're having a baby!" I exclaimed.

Charles jumped up and spun me around in his arms. We were a real family - Charles, Charlie, Domonique, this new baby and me.

Right Kind of Love

Francine Dupuy was born in April of 1971. I knew she was going to be a handful the minute she came out because she wouldn't stop whining and fussing. Even the nurse said, "It's going to take a lot to get this one to settle down." And that it did.

Mama came back again and, like before, she brought along my sister Franny, Francine's namesake. Franny was so excited to see Francine. The baby looked just like Franny. Unlike Charles, Francine had darker skin like me and dark brown eyes. Her little face was perfect and her head was topped with dark, curly hair.

Charlie loved his little sisters. He doted on them so much that sometimes I had to tell him to let them breathe. Domonique was walking now and getting into everything. Charles and I had our hands full. Mama and Franny stayed a few weeks. Franny wanted to stay longer but I told her that she needed to go back. She was still in high school and I wanted her to get her degree and go on to college. Buddy did what I had done and started working as soon as he graduated high school. Mama said he'd met some girl and was thinking about getting married. I was proud of Buddy, but I wanted more for Franny.

After Mama and Franny left it really hit me how much work I had to do now with three kids in the house. But I was happy to do it. I was content with my life. The road God led me down was not an easy one, but it sure brought me to a great place.

✱✱✱

A couple of weeks later we got a phone call from Sharon. Fred had been shot in combat. She was told that he wasn't dead, but they didn't say how badly he was injured. I prayed that Fred was ok. I could see in Charles' face how concerned he was for his friend. Though it was not how we wanted it to happen, Fred kept his word and he came home.

Charles and I went to see Fred in the hospital. We brought the kids but didn't tell Sharon that Domonique was Fred's daughter. When Fred saw Domonique his weary face lit up. I could see why. The older Domonique got, the more she looked like Vivian.

Fred sent Sharon on an errand so he could greet his daughter. When Sharon left he reached out his arms to hold Domonique. It was as if Domonique knew that he was her father because she went to him without fuss. Fred held her tightly in his arms and began to sob. "I thought I would never get to do this," he cried. "I thought I would never get to hold her."

"You have to tell Sharon," I said.

"I know," he replied as he covered Domonique with kisses.

"Where's…?" he started to ask.

I knew he was talking about Vivian. "We don't know."

"What are you gonna do now?" Charles asked him.

"I'm gonna get out this bed and get strong for my little girl," he said, his eyes glistening with tears.

And he did just that. Fred got up every morning and made it his business to get better. He'd gotten shot in his back near his spine and his legs didn't work that well. So he exercised and went through physical therapy to get stronger. He wasn't doing it for himself. He was doing it for Domonique.

Once he told Sharon about what happened between him and Vivian, she left him. But her love for Fred was stronger than we all knew because one night she came to the house to officially meet Domonique. Sharon cried at the sight of her. I had Charles stay with the kids in the living room while I took Sharon into the kitchen.

"How can I stay with him?" she asked through her tears.

"If you love him, it's easy," I replied.

"It's not whether I love him. It's whether he loves me," she said. "I've always known there was someone else. I just thought that he would see how much I loved him and that would be enough. But how can I compete with a baby?"

"You don't have to compete," I told her. "You and Fred need to decide where you want to go from here. Domonique ain't asking him to choose, so why should you? It's a lot, believe me, I know. But it's worth it for the right kind of love."

✳✳✳

A few weeks later the doorbell rang and it was Fred with a cane in one hand and Sharon's hand in the other. Domonique must have recognized him from all the times we took her to see him because she ran right up to him grabbing on to his leg. Fred laughed and, with Sharon's help, lifted Domonique into his arms.

She'd decided to stick it out and stay with Fred to work on their marriage. She said she realized that loving Fred meant loving Domonique and she was willing to do that. She said that she knew that Fred was worth it. I could tell that Vivian wasn't completely out of Fred's system, but I think having Domonique meant he had a little part of Vivian that would forever be his.

Fred and Sharon didn't want to uproot Domonique, and Charlie wasn't about to let them go far with her. So they found a house two doors down from where we lived. Francine and Domonique were still able to play together and Charlie got to keep an eye on both of his little sisters.

Best Part of Me

During the '80s, Fred and Sharon had gone on to have two boys of their own. Soon after he returned from Vietnam, Fred got a job at the Veteran's hospital and had worked there for years. The folks there had admired how hard he worked to get himself well after he was wounded. They had hired him as soon as he could start working. He helped young soldiers who came home with injuries.

The store was still hanging in there even though New York had changed over the years. Francine and Domonique were in middle school and Charlie was getting ready to start college. He came home saying he only applied to one college, the one his daddy wanted him to go to: Howard University. Charles was so proud to read that letter of acceptance. He hugged Charlie like he'd never let him go. Charlie was so smart and was turning into such a good man. Charles wasn't the only one proud of him.

I called Mama bragging. By that time she was living with Franny and her husband and children. Daddy had died of a heart attack. The biggest regret I ever had in my life was never making things right with Daddy. He never got to know my husband or meet my kids. He never got to see the amazing things God had done in my life. I missed Daddy every day and prayed that he managed to forgive me before he passed on.

As for Mama, she was ecstatic about Charlie. She wanted to put the news of him going to Howard University in the church newsletter and there was no talking her out of it. She and Charlie still had their daily talks and he still laughed at whatever she was telling him on the other end of the phone. Things were going well. We could afford to send our baby to college, thanks to Uncle Buck. My family was thriving. Everyone was happy.

Then out of the blue, we got an unexpected phone call. The woman on the other end said that she was a caseworker at a special kind of hospital that deals with terminally ill patients. She said that Vivian was one of those patients. My heart sank. I nearly dropped the phone.

Vivian had given her our number as her next-of-kin. The woman asked that I come down as soon as possible. She said she had to speak to me first before I could see Vivian. She said that she couldn't tell me much more over the phone. But I wanted to know more. Why was Vivian in there? And why couldn't she call herself? Or why did we have to meet with a caseworker before seeing her?

I held on to the receiver as if the caseworker would come back on and answer all my questions. But all I heard was a dial tone. I heard the door open and in walked Charlie, Charles and Fred. They saw the look on my face and knew something was wrong.

"What is it, Mae?" Charles asked, coming over to take the phone out of my hand.

"It's Vivian," I said and looked over at Fred.

"What is it?" Fred asked.

I told them what the woman said and suggested that we bring Domonique with us. Fred, Charles, Domonique and I went right over to that hospital and met with the caseworker.

She explained to us that there was an epidemic going around called Acquired Immune Deficiency Syndrome. She said Vivian had it, there was no cure, and she was in what they believed to be the final stages of the disease. They were expecting her to die at any minute. I started to shake. I could see the tears well up in Fred's eyes.

Domonique didn't seem to know how to feel and I couldn't blame her. She'd only heard us talk about Vivian. She'd never actually gotten to know her mother, and now it seemed she never will.

"How did she get this?" Fred asked.

"There are still studies being done, but the most common ways being reported are through homosexual activities or intravenous drug use. We think the latter is how she got it. According to our records, she has been a pretty heavy heroin user for many years," the woman explained.

I held my head in my hands. I felt like this was somehow my fault. If I hadn't kicked her out of the house then maybe she would have stopped using drugs and wouldn't have this disease.

When the woman walked us to Vivian's room she stopped at the closed door and turned to us. "Remember I said there are still tests being done on this disease. Therefore, we don't know all the ways it could be transmitted and because of that, you can't touch her and she knows not to touch you. You will also have to wear face masks." She handed each of us one of the white face masks that the doctors used. We put them on. Then she slowly opened the door and let us into Vivian's room.

I went in first, followed by Fred, with Domonique hiding behind him. Charles opted not to go in. He said what good would it do to see her like that. And he was right. Vivian was just a skeletal shell of herself. Her eyes were sunk into her head and there were sores all over her body. I wanted so badly to grab her and give her a hug. To hold her in my arms and tell her everything was going to be alright. But I was not allowed to touch her.

Vivian turned her head towards us and smiled, but it was clear she was in pain. She looked at Fred and then at frightened Domonique.

"Domonique," Vivian said softly. Domonique slowly came out from behind Fred and looked into her mother's eyes.

"Don't be scared, baby. I know I look a mess," Vivian said. "But they can tell you I didn't always look this way." Vivian tried to laugh but started coughing instead.

"She knows how beautiful you were…you are," I said to Vivian.

Vivian couldn't take her gaze off Domonique. The last time she saw her she was just a baby. I could see regret in her eyes.

"I'm sorry, baby," Vivian said to Domonique.

"For what?" Domonique asked.

"For being me. For letting you down. I swear I wanted to be the best mother to you, but I was weak and dumb," Vivian answered. She looked at Fred then back at Domonique. "The two of you were the best part of me."

I could see her hand shaking as she tried to keep from reaching out to Domonique. She wanted to touch her daughter one last time but she couldn't. Vivian had made many bad decisions in her life. But for this to be her end just didn't seem right.

"Please, promise me not to let her be like me," Vivian said to me and Fred.

"Viv…" Fred tried to say.

"No, Fred, promise me. Mae knows. It's a curse. My daddy was this way and I was just like him. But she can't be. She has to be different, she has to be unique. Please. Promise me," Vivian begged.

"We will, Viv," I said as Fred nodded his head yes in agreement.

"Wow," Vivian said, looking at Domonique again. "You're so beautiful."

"She looks just like you," Fred told her.

"Is this what you saw in me?" she asked him.

He smiled. "Yes."

"I wish I could have seen me through your eyes just once," she replied.

Fred reached over and grabbed Vivian by the hand. She tried to pull it away but he held on to her.

"Fred, you can't do that," I said to him.

"I'm doing it," he said. "I've never stopped loving you, Viv, and I never will."

Vivian used what little strength she had to squeeze his hand and said to him, "You want to know a secret?"

"What is it?" Fred asked with a smile.

"I think I loved you since the moment I laid eyes on you," she confessed.

"When we met backstage at *Buck's*?" Fred asked.

"No," she said. "When you walked *in*to *Buck's*. I saw you come in the front door while I was sitting at the bar and I said to myself, 'Wow. What a man.'"

Fred broke down in tears. He had waited so long for Vivian to say those words. Hearing them touched him somewhere deep in his soul. Domonique grabbed her father's other hand and stared at her mother. The moment was too intense for me and I ran out of the room crying and into Charles' arms.

A few days later, Vivian died from complications from Acquired Immune Deficiency Syndrome, or AIDS.

Things Happen

After Vivian's death, it took a little time before life felt normal again. The kids grew and went off to college. Domonique and Francine followed in Charlie's footsteps and went to Howard University which, of course, made Charles very happy.

Charles and I ended up selling the store because the neighborhood got a little too rough and there were a few break-ins. Besides, Charles had been working his entire life and he just wanted to be free to enjoy it for a bit.

Charlie came back to New York after he graduated college and went on to get his master's degree. Domonique also came back after college and became a social worker. She convinced Charlie to invest in a community center in the neighborhood they grew up in. She had done great things with that center. Francine decided that she was going to stay in D.C. She said there wasn't anything here for her in New York. That child worried me so much throughout the years, but Charles always said to let Fran be Fran. I didn't know what that meant. All I knew was that if I didn't bother Francine then she didn't have a reason to bother me.

My sister Franny and I talked almost every day over the phone. Buddy and I talked whenever we could. I made sure Charlie stayed close to his aunt, uncle, and cousins. I didn't see any reason why the family shouldn't stay close.

Mama died years ago in her sleep, just like Mrs. Polamo. I always figured that's the best way to go. No fuss, no pain, just peace. I miss Mama. I think Charlie took it the hardest. He didn't have his daily talks with her anymore. I told him I was still here and he could talk to me whenever he wanted.

Some years back Charles and I sat down with Charlie and told him about how he came into this world. I know we made a pact that we wouldn't tell anyone else, but we figured Charlie had the right to know. I cried when I told him, especially about how I treated him when he was first born. But my baby boy just hugged me and said he loved me anyhow. Then he apologized to me as if he had been the one to hurt me. I never could have imagined something so wonderful could come from something so horrible.

But nothing I'd been through could have prepared me for when I lost my Charles. I lost my soul. I thought I could be strong like Mrs. Polamo, but I wasn't. I just wanted him back. I didn't know why God left me on this earth without him. What else was left for me to do?

PART III

Easier Said Than Done

LaCrae pulled the covers over her grandmother as she slept. She knelt down beside her bed and looked around. Suddenly everything in the clustered room made sense. Even her grandfather's picture that looked onto the bed. She readjusted the scarf on her grandmother's head. Then she left the room, turning off the light on her way out.

LaCrae went into her bedroom and stared out the window. All that her grandmother had seen and done was way more than LaCrae could ever imagine. Her grandmother's life story played in her head like a recording. She smiled to herself at how trivial her issues were with Q compared to what her grandmother had been through. She made up her mind to make better choices for herself. There would be no more Q and his promises of dance stardom. If she wanted to continue to dance, she had to do it the right way. The problem was LaCrae didn't know what the right way was. Becoming the dancer she wanted to be seemed easier said than done.

✳✳✳

The next morning LaCrae woke up early and went to the community center just as Domonique was preparing to open the doors.

Dominque was surprised to see her. "Why are you here so early?"

"Is it too late?" LaCrae asked.

Domonique entered the center. "Too late for what?"

LaCrae clarified her question. "Too late to try out for the dance school?"

"No, not at all," Domonique replied with a smile. "I'll call my friend and see what she can do for you."

"Good," LaCrae said. "By the way, why didn't you tell me who you were?"

Domonique took a deep breath and sat down on a bench. "Would it have made a difference?" she asked.

"Well...I mean...I think so. We are related." LaCrae said. "I just thought you were this crazy lady who was all up in my business for no reason."

Domonique let out a loud laugh. "Well, I've been known to be all up in people's business whether I'm related to them or not. I'm guessing Aunty Mae filled you in."

"Yeah. She told me everything." LaCrae sat down next to Domonique on the bench and looked off into the distance.

Domonique smiled. "Your grandparents and my parents were a pretty great foursome, weren't they?"

"Yeah, I guess. Do you get mad at your mother for leaving you the way she did?" LaCrae asked.

Domonique thought for a minute. "No, not really. My mother was fighting demons that were in her way before she even met my father. I did and still do mourn the fact that I'll never get the opportunity to ask her what she did and what she went through during those years when she was away from me. But I can guess. I started a drug rehab program here and I see people who are strung out on drugs all the time. Sometimes I see my mother in them. I think not having me see her that way was probably the best gift she could have given me."

LaCrae let Domonique's word sink in. "So if you grew up with my mom and Uncle Charlie, why didn't I know you?"

"That's because your mother and I fell out when you were young. I actually came to visit her when you were born. Your mother and I are like sisters. We've been fighting since I could remember," Domonique explained. "So when we had that fight, I just assumed that it would blow over, we would eat ice cream and drink a glass of wine and that would be that. But it's been years and we still haven't spoken to each other. I miss her a lot."

"What did you guys fall out about?" LaCrae asked.

"I was the one who encouraged your dad to follow his dreams," Dominque told her. "Your dad was a great musician and I knew that if he didn't go after his dreams back then, he would end up resenting you and your mother. I just want the record to reflect that even though I was in her business, I was somewhat right."

"My dad left us," LaCrae pointed out.

"I heard. That's why I said I was somewhat right. My intentions were not to get him to leave, just to be a better husband and father," Domonique said. "I do have to learn to stay out of other people's business."

LaCrae sat and talked to Domonique for a while before heading back home. She ran into the house when she saw her uncle's car parked out front. She had a lot to talk to him about and she needed answers to several questions. She found her aunt and uncle talking at the kitchen table.

"Uncle Charlie!" LaCrae said.

"What is it, LaCrae? Is everything alright?" he asked.

"Grandma told me everything."

Charlie looked at her, grinning. Then he said, "She is one incredible woman, isn't she?"

"Yeah she is," LaCrae agreed. "But we got to make things right with her and my mother before..."

"Before what?" he asked her.

"I know she's sick, Uncle Charlie," LaCrae told him.

Charlie looked over at Esther, their expressions full of sadness.

"What?" LaCrae asked.

"She's sicker than you think, LaCrae. The cancer is in its final stages and she's refusing any more medication. The kind of time that's needed for your mom and grandmother to fix their issues just isn't there," he told her.

"But Grandma said that her biggest regret was not fixing things with her dad before he died. I don't want that to be my mother's biggest regret, too. Uncle Charlie, she doesn't know all the things that you and I know about Grandma. I think she should know," LaCrae said.

"I agree with you, LaCrae, but it is your grandmother's story to tell. Just like she chose to tell you, she has to choose to tell Fran."

LaCrae wasn't satisfied with her uncle's response. She knew that things wouldn't be right with her family until her mother knew the whole story. She went into her grandmother's room.

"Hey, baby," Mae said softly. "What's that in your hand?" Mae pointed at the pad of paper and pen that

LaCrae had partially hidden behind her back. She found it laying on the desk by the phone in the living room.

LaCrae handed her the pad and pen. "Grandma, I think you should write my mom a letter. I think it's time she got to know you like I do now." Then she left the room to rejoin her aunt and uncle downstairs.

She announced to them that she was going to try out for the Dance Academy in a few weeks and then she ran out the door. Charlie and Esther laughed at this good news, relieved to hear her decision. They were proud of their niece.

LaCrae ran down to the basement apartment and knocked on the door. When Julio answered she launched herself into his arms and kissed him.

"What was that for?" Julio asked when they broke apart, a huge smile on his face.

She smiled back at him. "Just thought it was about time. Why wait?"

What God Intended

LaCrae spent the next few days taking care of Mae and practicing for tryouts. She had grown to love talking to her grandmother and couldn't wait to run home to be with her. LaCrae had learned what was important in life. She vowed to never live her life selfishly or chase the wrong things. She was determined to get into the Dance Academy and everyone around her wanted the same.

Mae told her to dance not for the judges but for herself. To reach deep down inside and bring forth a talent that only God knew existed. That was exactly what LaCrae intended to do.

"If you could have, Grandma, would you have been that big star? I mean, if everything didn't happen the way it did?" LaCrae asked. Mae laid on the sofa, weakened due to her illness.

"I don't know. I think things happened as they should. I think me coming to New York was about more than me signing and being a big star. I found love and I built a family. Now my granddaughter will be dancing on the Apollo stage. I think I did exactly what God intended for me to do," Mae explained.

"But, could you see yourself on that Apollo stage?" LaCrae asked.

"Oh, I saw myself on many stages. But what I want most is to be in Charles' arms again. At the end of your journey, child, all that matters is that you end up in the place that makes you happy. I can't wait until I get there." Mae sighed deeply and fell asleep.

LaCrae gazed out the window as the living room grew quiet. The lights seemed to dim and her grandmother's song began to softly play in the background. LaCrae quickly looked around to see who turned on the music. Other than Mae, no one else was in the house. Then a bright, white light came through the ceiling and landed in the middle of the living room floor. A male figure appeared. LaCrae froze. She had no idea what was happening.

The figure stood over the sofa where Mae was laying and held out his hand. Mae took it and stood up. The two of them embraced and it was then that LaCrae realized that the figure was her grandfather. Her grandparents held each other tight as they danced into the white light. And then the light was gone, the music stopped, and the living room was quiet again.

LaCrae got up and slowly walked over to the sofa. Her grandmother was lying there, motionless, a slight smile on her face. LaCrae kissed her and said, "Bye, Grandma. Thank you for everything."

No Need for Regret

The day of Mae's funeral seemed to come quickly. Charlie, Esther, and Domonique planned the service. Mae didn't want any fuss, she just wanted to be laid to rest next to her husband.

LaCrae was up in her room getting ready for the funeral when she saw a cab pull up in front of the house. Fran emerged from the back seat. LaCrae ran down the stairs to tell everyone that her mother had arrived. They looked at each other as if to prepare themselves for what was about to happen. LaCrae opened the front door. Francine stood there, dressed in all black with a hat on her head.

"Hi, Mom," LaCrae said, reaching out to give her a hug.

"Hello, LaCrae," Francine replied. She was still upset with LaCrae.

Francine walked into the house and looked around. It had been years since she'd been back. Everything seemed strange and unfamiliar to her.

"Hey, sis," Charlie said as he ran over to give Francine a hug.

"Hello, Francine," Esther said.

Francine hugged her brother and nodded her head toward Esther. She looked behind Esther and saw Domonique standing there. "Well, I see the gang's all here." She walked into the living room to sit down.

At that moment, Julio arrived dressed in his black suit. He greeted LaCrae with a kiss. Francine was livid.

"So, you came here to get a man, I see," Francine said to LaCrae.

"No, Mom," LaCrae said, lowering her head in embarrassment. "This is -,"

"Hi, Ms. Dupuy. I'm Julio." He intervened, realizing that LaCrae was nervous. He stuck out his hand for Francine to shake, but she just stared at it. Charlie walked over and grabbed Julio's hand instead.

"Glad you could make it, son," Charlie said.

They waited for Charlie and Esther's children to arrive. Then they all got into a black limousine that was sent by the funeral home and went to the church for the service. It seemed like the whole neighborhood was there. It was the first time LaCrae saw her uncle cry. Julio put his arm around LaCrae and held on to her. Francine put on her shades to help maintain her stoic expression.

An older man and woman walked into the church and right up to the front. Charlie stood up to embrace them. "Aunt Franny, Uncle Buddy. Glad you guys could make it."

LaCrae noticed her mother perk up. Francine got up and ran right into the arms of Franny.

Later at the gravesite, LaCrae was standing by Domonique when Fran walked up to her. At first, LaCrae thought that the sadness of the day had finally gotten to her and she was ready to embrace everyone. But that was not the case.

"LaCrae, I see you found some people here in New York who would have been better off if they remained missing," Francine said, directing her attention towards LaCrae but her comment at Domonique.

"I never went missing, Fran," Domonique replied. "You just decided I wasn't worth being around."

"So, is that what's been going on here? You've all been filling my daughter's head with lies? As if I'm the bad person?" Francine asked. "Did you tell her how you ruined her family?"

"Fran, at this point LaCrae knows more than you. So perhaps you need to get a clue from her and when you're ready to be my sister again, I'll be here." Domonique walked away.

"Mom, why did you do that?" LaCrae asked.

"Do what?" Francine asked, feigning innocence.

"What you always do! You're always so mean and harsh towards everyone," LaCrae said.

"Oh, so I was right," Francine said. "They have poisoned your view of me."

"No one can ever poison me against you. I love you, Mom, but you've got to stop," LaCrae said.

"LaCrae…I…" Francine began, fighting back her anger.

"Mom, Grandma's dead and the two of you never got to say to each other all the things you should have. Won't you regret that?"

"If your grandmother had anything she needed to tell me she would have, I'm sure of it. There's no need for regret," Francine reasoned.

"But she did." LaCrae pulled out a white envelope and handed it to Francine. She had gone into her grandmother's room the day before the funeral and found the envelope sitting on the nightstand. It was addressed to Francine. Francine took the letter and stared at it.

LaCrae turned to leave but stopped. She looked back at her mother. "I'm auditioning for the Dance Academy tomorrow morning at the Apollo Theater. They're going to allow people to sit in the audience and watch. Everyone's coming and I really hope you can be there." She gave her a hug and walked away.

Momma, Oh Momma!

It was early the next morning and Francine was gathering her things to check out of the hotel and head to the airport. The letter from her mother was sitting on the desk by the lamp. She had meant to read it before going to bed but just couldn't bring herself to do so. Francine picked up the letter and stuffed it in her purse. She grabbed her luggage and headed out the door.

After checking out, the concierge hailed a cab for her. She told the driver to take her to the airport. LaCrae's audition would be starting soon, but she had no intention of being there to see her daughter destroy her life. As the cab started moving Francine pulled the letter out of her purse and opened it.

My Dearest Francine,

You and I have butted heads so often throughout the years. But I love you more than you will ever know. You are the child created by love. Your father was my soul and you are a living, breathing reminder of what our love meant. I know you felt like I treated you differently and perhaps I did. But it had nothing to do with you, and everything to do with me. I was hurt badly. I watched others hurt, sometimes by their own doing. I just didn't want you to have to go through the same thing.

You see, Charlie, while I love him to my core, was brought into this world through violence and darkness. I was raped when I was not much older than LaCrae because I was chasing a dream that was never meant for me. Because of that, I raised you to do the opposite. I wanted you to be such a strong woman that nothing, not even the darkest of evils, could ever hurt you. I didn't want what happened to me to happen to you. But in doing that I taught you how to be closed off from the world, how not to trust anyone. And somehow you got the message that you didn't matter to me. But baby, you mattered. I looked at you and I saw the love that God sent my way. The love that saved me over and over again. The love that brought me back from the brink of despair. I'm so sorry if I ever made you feel anything less than a loved child.

You were my only chance to experience what it was like to have true love growing inside of me, and for that, I am grateful to you. We never get a chance to go back and fix the mistakes of the past but we are granted the opportunity to change the future. Do not have the relationship with LaCrae that we had. Do not let her go through life thinking that you being right is more important than you loving her unconditionally.

I never got a chance to make things right with my father. You and I never got a chance to make things right. But my sweet baby girl, you and LaCrae have that chance. Please don't waste it. She's a good girl with a good head on her shoulders. But she has big dreams and needs someone there to make sure she reaches her dreams the right way.

I love you, dear Fran, my love child. Go on in life and be happy knowing that you are loved and that you were made from love. No one will ever be able to take that away from you.

Love,

Momma

Francine squeezed the letter against her chest, overcome with emotion. Sobs shook her body as she cried out, "MOMMA! OH, MOMMA!"

For You, Grandma

LaCrae sat backstage at the Apollo Theater with hundreds of other girls who all wanted the same thing. She was nervous, but she tried to relax as she stretched. She wished her grandmother was there to see her, but LaCrae could still feel her presence within.

Julio snuck backstage and came over to check on her.

"What are you doing here?" LaCrae asked, excited to see him.

"I just want to wish you good luck. I know you're going to kill it," he said, pulling her into a hug.

LaCrae held on to Julio until she heard them call her number. He gave her a smile and a wink as she made her way to the stage. She could see her aunt, uncle, and Domonique sitting in the theater, silently cheering her on by giving her the thumbs up sign and big smiles. Then the doors at the back of the theater opened.

Francine walked in. She looked at LaCrae on the stage and blew her a kiss. She hurried to sit down next to Domonique and held her hand.

LaCrae couldn't stop the smile that spread across her face. The music started and Mae's voice began to sing. She looked out across the auditorium and saw her grandmother standing there in her fancy, yellow dress with a flower in her hair.

"This is for you, Grandma," LaCrae said out loud as she started to dance. It seemed like she and her grandmother were the only people in the entire theater. Mae sang and LaCrae danced from a place that only God knew existed.

She finished as the music stopped and turned towards her grandmother. Mae smiled at her and disappeared. LaCrae looked into the audience to see her whole family, including her mother, cheering for her as they clapped their hands and screamed her name. Julio ran onto the stage, picked her up and swung her around. He sat her down again and she noticed the judges whispering among themselves.

And then, one of them said, "LaCrae James. Welcome to the Dance Academy."

THE END